DARING TO
DATE HER EX

BY
ANNIE CLAYDON

MILLS
BOON

Published in Great Britain 2015
by Mills & Boon, an imprint of Harlequin (UK) Limited,
Eton House, 18-24 Paradise Road, Richmond, Surrey, TW9 1SR

© 2015 Annie Claydon

ISBN: 978-0-263-24707-7

Printed and bound in Spain
by CPI, Barcelona

Cursed from an early age with a poor sense of direction and a propensity to read, **Annie Claydon** spent much of her childhood lost in books. After completing her degree in English Literature she indulged her love of romantic fiction and spent a long, hot summer writing a book of her own. It was duly rejected and life took over. A series of U-turns led in the unlikely direction of a career in computing and information technology, but the lure of the printed page proved too much to bear and she now has the perfect outlet for the stories which have always run through her head: writing Medical Romance™ for Mills & Boon®. Living in London—a city where getting lost can be a joy—she has no regrets for having taken her time in working her way back to the place that she started from.

Books by Annie Claydon

**Please visit the author profile page
at millsandboon.co.uk for more titles**

To all the readers, editors, family and friends
who've supported me this far.
Thank you.

PROLOGUE

HE WASN'T THERE.

Thea Coleman surveyed the sea of heads bobbing in front of her. No reason to panic. There were walkways, coffee shops, seating areas to check out... It had been a nice fantasy, stepping out of a taxi and bumping into Lucas almost straight away. Seeing his face light up when he saw her, holding his hand as they walked together into the airport to embark on the biggest adventure of their lives. But fantasy was a forgiving and flexible thing, and there was another one that would do just as well. Finding him at the last minute, just as he was about to board the plane. Pushing through the crowds to fling herself into his arms, and flying off into the sunset with him.

She checked her luggage in, went through passport control, and scanned the passenger lounge anxiously. It looked as if fantasy number three was going to be the one. She'd find him on the plane. Lucas would have given up all hope that she might change her mind and come with him by then.

She knew that he was on this flight; the tickets had been propped up in front of the mirror in his bedroom for over a month. Every night she'd offered up the silent hope that he might change his mind. That he'd ask her to put her career on hold and go with him. Or that he'd decide that the opportunity of working as a doctor in Bangladesh was a dream he could postpone until she had completed her two years' foundation training and could apply to work alongside him.

Every morning the tickets had still been there and there was one less day to count before he used them. It would be sensible to wave him goodbye and get on with her life. Only love didn't listen to sense.

As soon as the seat-belt light dinged off, she squeezed past the man sitting next to her and walked up and down the aisles of the plane. Slipped into business class, in case he'd got an upgrade, and managed to ascertain that he wasn't there before she was politely asked to leave by one of the flight attendants. When the plane landed in Dhaka, she had no more fantasies left to rely on.

She tried not to cry as she went through passport control and claimed her baggage. Covering her long, fair hair with a scarf, she walked out of the airport alone into the unforgiving heat of an unknown city.

CHAPTER ONE

Seven years later—Day One

THERE WAS NOTHING especially urgent about the manner in which the phone rang, but context was everything. Not many people called at seven o'clock on a Monday morning for an idle chat. And it was one of the laws of the universe that you could come into work early, hoping for a couple of quiet hours before the switchboard opened at nine, and something would happen.

Thea reached for the phone. 'Dr Coleman.'

'Good. Glad you're here...'

'What is it, Jake?' She surveyed the carefully ordered pile of paperwork in front of her. In comparison to the sometimes chaotic disorder of the Central London A and E department downstairs, it suddenly seemed like a poor shadow of reality.

'I've got a thirty-four-year-old male that I want a second opinion on. Will you come and have a look?'

'I'll be right down.' Paperwork might be a necessity, but it didn't put a smile on her face when she got out of bed in the morning. And Thea was smiling as she put the phone down.

'Where is everybody?'

Jake Turner was a great guy and a good doctor, but he

generally didn't have much of an appreciation of time. A busy shift in A and E could do that to you.

'It's seven in the morning, Jake. Anyone with any sense is still thinking about getting out of bed.'

'Ah. No wonder I had to ring around.'

'You mean you didn't call me first? I'm devastated.'

Jake snorted with laughter. 'I tried Michael Freeman. I thought he'd want to know about this.'

Michael was Head of Respiratory Medicine at the hospital. 'So what have you got that warranted the attention of our beloved leader? I don't see any holes in the walls or visiting dignitaries.'

'Thirty-four-year-old male, persistent cough, congested lungs and recent weight loss. I've had some X-rays done and I think it might be tuberculosis.'

'What's his history?'

'He's been sick for a while. His GP put him on antibiotics and he improved a bit then deteriorated again after he finished them. He came in last night with chest pains and difficulty breathing.'

Thea flipped through the A and E notes that Jake had handed her. 'Any travel overseas lately?'

'Nope, nothing. And this guy's a teacher.'

'From…'

'The big secondary school up the road.'

Something pricked at the back of Thea's neck. A couple of thousand pupils, aged eleven to eighteen, all crammed into an overcrowded inner-city school. Along with a suspected case of TB. 'Great. You'd better be wrong, Jake.'

Unlikely. Jake was far too good a doctor for that.

'Yeah. Let's hope so.'

Mr Michael Freeman, Head of Respiratory Medicine, leaned back in his leather chair, rubbing his neck as if it hurt. 'You're sure?'

'Sure as I can be. I've put a rush on the initial tests and

we should have them back within twenty-four hours. But the patient has all the symptoms of active pulmonary TB.' Thea slipped the X-rays out of their sleeve and clipped them into the light box on the wall.

Michael studied them carefully. 'I agree. You're admitting him?'

'Yes, I want to keep him under observation for a few days.' Thea pointed to the areas on the X-ray that indicated fluid in the patient's pleural cavity. 'The pleural effusion might well resolve once we start medication, but if it gets any worse I'll need to do a thoracentesis.'

'I agree. I want you to supervise the isolation procedures yourself, along with the notifications. If we have a situation where the infection's already spread, then I want you dealing with it.'

'I hope it hasn't.'

Michael fell back into his chair. 'So do I. What do you think, though? Worst-case scenario.'

This was Michael's preferred modus operandi. He knew the answers already and, as the head of department, it was his job to make the decisions. But he always listened to his staff, and let them come up with the solutions he already had in mind.

'Given that TB's not that infectious…' Thea let out a sigh. False optimism wasn't going to help the situation. 'Worst-case scenario is that we have an unknown number of pupils infected. The patient's not been abroad in the last five years so the source of his infection is probably in this area. The contact tracing's going to be a big job and we'll have to do it carefully. We don't want wide-scale panic, but we do want to provide prompt testing where it's appropriate.'

Michael nodded. 'Agreed. And what do you recommend for resourcing?'

'We can't do it all ourselves. We'll need consultancy

from Public Health England, and probably a couple of extra
TB nurses to support the staff here.'

'Any ideas about who might be leading the hospital
team?'

'I'd thought that you would be doing that.'

Michael gave her the smile that he usually reserved for
anyone who wasn't quite catching his drift. 'I see from
your staff record that you worked in Bangladesh for two
years at a TB clinic.'

'That was three years ago.' Thea never talked about
Bangladesh. She was surprised that Michael even knew
she'd been there, but she supposed her CV must be on file
somewhere.

'Are you telling me you've forgotten what you learned
there?'

She would never forget. The suffering she'd seen at a
TB clinic, during her first short trip, had drowned out the
clamour of her own breaking heart. Lucas's dream had become hers, and she'd known she'd have to return.

Two years later, she'd realised that dream and travelled
to Bangladesh to work. And then the traumatic, unforget-
table lesson that had destroyed everything and brought her
back home. But that was history now. She had to move on.

'If you're planning to have someone else lead the hospital team, then I'd like you to consider me as a candidate.
I think I'm qualified to do it.'

Michael nodded, his self-satisfied smirk a sure indication that the conversation was going the way he wanted it
to. 'I'm glad you think so, because I was considering offering you the position. It's conditional, though.'

'What's the condition?' Something about the way that
Michael said it warned Thea that she wasn't going to like it.

'The conference I spoke about last week. The one you've
expressed no interest in.'

Thea's heart sank. 'The one in Mumbai, where you've

been asked to present a paper on the spread of TB in inner London.'

'That's the one. Only the request was for a representative of this department to present a paper. My name wasn't mentioned.' Michael paused, looking at her steadily. 'Most people would jump at the chance.'

Thea wasn't most people. 'I thought it went without saying that it should be you. You represent the department.'

'I *lead* the department. Which means it's my job to encourage my staff to realise their full potential.' Michael leaned back in his chair. 'It's up to you. If you want to head up the team you have to be prepared to share what you learn, and the conference will be good experience for you. Take it or leave it.'

She wouldn't get another opportunity like this again. If she really cared about what she did… There were so many reasons for saying yes, but they still couldn't crowd out the dread that accompanied the thought of standing up in front of a lecture hall full of people.

'I'll take it.' The words almost stuck in her throat, but she managed to get them out.

'Good. In that case, I want you to keep me in the loop and let me know what resources you'll need.'

'Thank you.' She may as well start now. 'With regard to the testing at the school, we may well be able to do that in a few weeks' time.'

'Why's that?' Michael knew as well as she did that best practice would be to wait for ten weeks, the incubation period for TB.

'The patient's been off work sick for a while. He was diagnosed as having pneumonia and was at home for three weeks before Easter. His GP gave him antibiotics and he responded to those, but he didn't go straight back to work because it was only a few days until the end of term. His condition got worse again after Easter, and he hasn't been back to work since.'

'So that's…how long?'

'No contact with any of his pupils for seven weeks now.'

Michael nodded. 'In some ways that's a blessing. We won't be besieged by parents, wanting to know why their kids aren't being tested immediately.'

'Yes, but we'll…' Thea grinned. 'I mean *I'll* have my work cut out to get all the contacts notified and everything in place for when the testing does start.'

'Then make sure that you use all of the support that's available from outside agencies. Do you need any help with your other caseload?'

'Not at the moment, but I'd like to keep that offer in hand. And I want to give some thought to where we'll seat the team and do the testing. I want to set up a separate clinic.'

Michael nodded in approval. 'All right. Let me know when you've decided and I'll deal with the red tape.'

Thea already had somewhere in mind but she needed to see her patient first. 'Thanks. Is after lunch any good for you?'

'I have some time at one o'clock. If that's soon enough for you.' Michael gave her an amused look, which Thea ignored. He'd given her this job, and she was going to prove to him, beyond all question, that he'd made the right choice.

Dr Lucas West drove through the main entrance of the hospital and down the ramp into the underground car park. He was not supposed to be here until tomorrow morning but his afternoon meeting had ended early, and in his experience one could learn a lot about a place by just wandering in unannounced at the end of a working day. He wanted to see the way that Michael Freeman's department ran when it *wasn't* expecting a visit.

And the fax he'd received that morning was worrying. A case of tuberculosis was always a matter of concern, but

a teacher in a large, inner-city school demanded his immediate attention.

The hospital was fifty years old, built with all the ir-
repressible optimism of the nineteen sixties. Since then it
had clearly taken a few knocks, and although Lucas noted
that it was scrupulously clean, he also saw that it was out-
dated in places and groaning under the number of people
that it served.

He also noted that the receptionist in the department for
respiratory medicine directed him back downstairs again,
when he identified himself as a consultant, sent by PHE.
He would have to have a word with whoever was in charge
here. Clearly no one had thought much about the logistics
of having a potentially large number of clinic attendees
walking from one end of the hospital to the other and then
back again to find the place they were meant to be going.

He found the room number he'd been directed to at the
end of a long, dingy corridor. Ignoring the 'Please Knock
and Wait' sign taped to the door, he walked straight in,
the door handle turning and then coming off in his hand.

She'd cut her hair.

Suddenly every thought, each one of his resolutions to
sort this mess out, was blanked from his mind. There was
nothing else other than the unexpected realisation that Thea
had cut her beautiful hair.

For a moment she didn't recognise him. That hurt even
more than the corruption of the memory of Thea's corn-
coloured hair spread out like liquid sunshine.

'Thea.' He supposed he should say more, but right now
that wasn't an option.

'Lucas.' She seemed to be coping with the moment better than he was. Or perhaps that was just what he wanted to
think. He was probably just a distant memory to her, and
there was nothing for her to cope with.

She walked towards him, stretching out her hand, more
self-possessed than she'd been seven years ago. Thea had

clearly learned to conceal her feelings, and that was yet another loss. Seven years ago she would have either rushed to hug him or aimed a punch at him. Either would have been better than this.

'My door handle.'

'Oh… Yes.' He dropped the handle into her palm, careful not to brush his fingers against hers.

'Thank you.' She turned away, as if that was the only thing that interested her about him, and picked up a screwdriver from the windowsill.

Lucas reminded himself what he'd come here to do, and where in the chain of command he intended to be. 'I'm here to see Michael Freeman. He's co-ordinating the TB response team.'

She nodded, slipping past him and kneeling in front of the open door. 'No, I am. Put your foot there, will you?'

Lucas planted his foot against the door, holding it steady while she applied herself to screwing the handle back on again. 'I'm the consultant from PHE.'

The words generally had some effect on people, but they barely seemed to register. She gave a brief nod and yanked brutally at the door handle to test that it was now securely fixed.

He had to stop this now. Thea didn't seem to have any understanding of the gravity of the task ahead of them, and if she thought he was here to act as apprentice handyman it was time to disillusion her. 'Isn't there someone else who can do this? We both have more important issues to deal with.'

She looked up at him for a moment. Her eyes were the same, dark and thoughtful, eyes that you could lose yourself in. That he *had* lost himself in once, on a very regular basis. Right now a spark of fire, or maybe just a trick of the light, turned brown to gold.

'I could walk upstairs, find a requisition form, and wait two days for someone from Maintenance to come and fix it.

And if you were going to turn up unannounced, you could at least have read the notice on the door...' She got to her feet and turned away from him again.

Annoyance gripped at his chest. Thea had never just walked away from him like that before, and it surprised Lucas that it was no easier to take now than it would have been seven years ago. The impulse to spin her round, take her off balance and kiss her rose from his heart to his head, and his head dismissed it out of hand.

The roaring in his ears began to subside and professionalism took over. This was just another situation that he had to get on top of, and he had never failed to win hearts and minds when he needed to. Lucas put his briefcase down at his feet and knocked gently on the open door. She took her time in turning to face him, but when she did a touch of humour was tugging at her mouth.

'Dr Lucas West. I'm looking for the head of the TB response team.'

'Dr Thea Coleman. You've come to the right place.'

They didn't shake hands. It was probably best not to touch her just yet.

'You look well, Thea.' It was a pleasantry rather than a compliment. She seemed paler than he remembered her, and grey didn't suit her as well as the vibrant colours she used to wear. Lucas pressed on. 'Do you have some time to talk?'

She nodded. 'Of course. Why don't we go for coffee?'

He smiled at her. Thea had always been able to make him smile, even now. 'That sounds good.'

One word had sounded at the back of her head, forming a long scream of disbelief. *No-o-o.*

It had taken every ounce of Thea's self-control not to run from the room. Lucas had taught her how to love and had then left her. Seven years, several oceans, and a lot of water under the bridge later, here he was. His dark hair a little shorter, and definitely tidier. Wearing a suit, of all things.

A cold detachment, as if she'd taken a step back from the world and was no longer a part of it, came to her rescue. Someone else had taken the door handle from him and answered him back, while the real Thea had been shivering in a corner, screaming that this could not be happening.

'How have you been?' He followed her through the canteen and into the garden beyond, putting his coffee down on the bench between them.

'Fine. You?'

He nodded. 'Fine.'

That seemed to cover their personal lives for the past seven years. If he'd followed even a few of the dreams that he'd shared with her over the two years they'd been together, it was unlikely that his professional life had been as uneventful.

'You have experience of dealing with TB abroad?'

Something tightened his face into a mask. 'I didn't go abroad. Things happened…'

He seemed disinclined to say what things could possibly have got in the way of what he'd considered his destiny. 'I worked at a TB clinic in the UK for a while and now I consult. Better hours…'

He stopped short as Thea choked on her coffee. The Lucas she'd known hadn't owned a suit and had cared nothing for regular hours.

'Are you okay?'

He looked as if he was about to thump her on the back. 'Yes, fine…' Thea waved him away. 'Where was the TB clinic?'

'South London.' He seemed to recognise the awkwardness of the admission and changed the subject quickly. 'You've been working here since you qualified?'

'No, three years.' The other four were none of his business. Thea could practically feel herself retreating again behind the protective shell that she had learned to cloak herself with in the hard weeks before her return from Bangladesh. The Lucas that she'd known had been charming and unconventional, an idealist and totally committed to his goals. There was nothing of that man here.

She stared hard at a clump of daisies in the grass at her feet, fighting for control. 'I'll let you have the case notes for the patient we have here at the hospital. You might like to see him.'

He nodded, as if he understood that Thea had nothing more of a personal nature left to say. 'Yes, that would be good. You're thinking of working out of the room on the ground floor?'

'Yes.'

'It's not very well signposted, and it's a way away from the department. We may have to review that location at our first team meeting tomorrow morning. Can you come up with some alternatives, or should I speak with your head of department about that?'

Like hell he would. 'You can speak to me. I'm the liaison officer.'

He gave a small nod. 'In that case, I'd like to see some alternatives. Preferably in the department and with easy, well-signposted access. It looks as if we may be testing a large number of contacts, and I don't want people having to wander around the way I did.'

'I chose the clinic on the ground floor because it has its own separate external entrance, which is a hundred metres from the bus stop in the hospital grounds.'

'But if you come in at the main gates—'

'No one does, unless they're driving. The back gates are five minutes from the school. The department's senior secretary is preparing a map that we can append to all the appointment letters, and she'll get some temporary signage as soon as we agree on wording.'

'And access to the department?'

This must be new territory for Lucas. Seven years ago, Thea had usually been the one to back down, in the face of two years' seniority in their studies and Lucas's seductive charm. Things were different now.

'There's a stairway between us and the department. We have easy access to the X-ray department, and there's a counselling suite next door, which I can annex for our use if we need it.'

'You seem to have all the answers.'

Not by a very long way. But she knew her own hospital better than he did at least. 'It's agreed, then?'

A smile twitched at the side of his mouth, and Thea ignored it. 'Yes. Agreed.'

CHAPTER TWO

Day Two

THE MEETING CONVENED at eight o'clock the next morning, with Lucas sitting at the head of the table as if he owned it. He was indisputably at the helm, guiding them through the long agenda with the minimum of fuss. When Lucas put his mind to something, Thea had never seen him fail.

'My office.' Michael gathered up his papers from the desk, murmuring the words as he walked behind Thea towards the door, and she followed him out of the room. Her professionalism had slipped just once that morning. Lucas had made a joke and she'd responded a little too quickly and with a bit too much bite. It wouldn't happen again but Michael didn't miss much.

'Any concerns?' Michael had closed the door of his office behind them and waved her to a seat.

'I don't think so. This is much as I'd expected—'

'You know Dr West?'

'Yes.' Thea gave up the pretence that she'd been clinging to all morning. She supposed that it would all come out sooner or later anyway. 'I know him. He worked at the hospital where I trained.'

Michael nodded her on. He obviously wasn't done yet, and it was unlikely he'd let her out of here until he was.

'We went out for a while. Two years, actually. I haven't seen him since then.'

'Hmm.' Michael was obviously weighing up the information. 'Ran its course?'

'He had plans to work abroad. I'd only just finished medical school and had my two years' foundation training still to do. I had my career to consider.'

Michael looked about as convinced as Thea felt that this was all there was to it. 'Okay. I won't pry any further into things that don't concern me. All I really need to know is whether you can work with him effectively.'

Thea had been willing to put her career on hold for Lucas once. Once was enough. She wasn't going to lose this job over something that had been over for seven years.

'I always had a great deal of respect for Lucas's abilities and I still do. I'm qualified for this job, and I want to do it well. I'm confident that the same goes for him.'

'All right.' Michael leaned back in his chair, a flip of his hand indicating that she was off the hook. 'Go do it. Remember that my door's always open.'

Lucas hadn't failed to notice that Thea had followed her boss out of the conference room, probably responding from some signal from Michael. They'd been gone for ten minutes now, and he guessed that they were talking about him.

Fair enough. It was pretty much par for the course that everyone talked about an external consultant, weighing him up, deciding how capable he was. Lucas took it for granted and concentrated on proving himself. But this was different. He was half expecting to be summoned to Michael Freeman's office and discreetly informed that Thea would no longer be working directly with him, as if he posed some kind of threat to her.

He waited. The half-open door of the conference room suddenly swung wide and Thea was in the doorway. 'I've just spoken with Michael's secretary. The microbiology results are in.'

There was an assurance in her face that said that something had been discussed and a decision made. Whatever the details, Lucas couldn't help but applaud the outcome, because it had brought her back to him.

Responding to a silent alert, she consulted her pager. 'Sorry, got to go. I'm needed up on the ward.'

'Our TB case?' When she nodded her assent, he picked up his papers and buttoned his jacket. He had heard all about the isolation procedures and the patient's condition at the meeting, but he wanted to check on both. 'I'll walk with you.'

Lucas fell into step beside her, following her through the twists and turns of the hospital corridors. She was walking so fast that he had to lengthen his stride to keep up with her. 'Microbiology?' Lucas reminded her.

'Ah, yes. It's been confirmed as TB—a partially drug-resistant strain, which has markers in common with a known strain found in the Birmingham area a year ago.'

'I'll get the notes on which drug regime worked best there. The patient has contacts in Birmingham?'

'Not as far as I know. We got some details from the wife, but I was reckoning on interviewing her more fully after we'd liaised with you.' She smiled suddenly and the Thea he knew broke from the shell of the woman she'd become. Eager for the task ahead and ready to face its challenges.

After the bustling hospital corridors, the isolation suite was like an oasis of regulated calm. A nursing station gave access to four separate rooms, each entered via a small lobby. Dispensers at each door held protective masks, gloves and aprons.

Automatically, Lucas's gaze flipped to the pressure gauge at the side of the door. In order to eliminate the spread of airborne particles containing mycobacterium tuberculosis, the room should be kept under negative pressure.

It was. The whole place seemed to exude a smug pride, telling him he could look as hard as he liked, everything was being done by the book. Quiet and efficient, even if the masks and aprons of the nursing staff did lend an impersonal touch.

And then there was Thea. She approached the man in the bed, who was coughing painfully and being supported in a sitting position by a nurse. Lucas could hear the scrape of lungs that couldn't do their job properly screaming for air.

'Hey, there, Derek.' Despite the mask, Lucas could see her smile. It leaked out of her, in her posture, the way she touched the back of his hand with her gloved fingertips. Her eyes. It struck Lucas that if the last thing he ever saw was her eyes, warm and full of compassion, then he'd be a happy man.

'Not so good today, I see.' Derek was fighting for breath and so Thea voiced both sides of the conversation. 'Okay, let's have a listen to your chest.'

She nodded to the nurse, who helped her pull the gown away from Derek's back. A careful, thorough examination seemed to confirm what was already obvious. Overnight, Derek's condition had deteriorated, and the fluid on his lungs was now making it painful and difficult to breathe.

'Good. You're doing great.' Thea helped the nurse settle Derek back onto the pillows. 'I think that we can make you more comfortable, though.'

That smile again. And suddenly, in response, Derek's face seemed to throw off the anonymity of pain. He was no longer just a patient, defined by what treatment the hospital could give. He was a man in his thirties, sandy hair, blue eyes. Who had a wife and a job and a life outside these walls.

And a sense of humour. Thea made a joke, the nurse laughed, and Derek's eyes suddenly lit up. She patted his hand and gave him a wave, before sweeping out of the room, leaving Lucas to follow her.

Outside, she was all business. Standing by the glazed wall of the isolation room so that Derek could see she was still there, she looked up at Lucas, her gaze serious.

'I was hoping that the pleural effusion would stay stable.'

'We need to do a thoracentesis.' Lucas provided the obvious answer. 'You have a mobile ultrasound unit available?'

'Yes. I'll get it up here.'

'The sooner the better. I think we should consider a drain as well.'

She nodded.

'He has no blood coagulation issues?'

'No. And he understands what's happening and is co-operative. We can keep him calm while we do the procedure.'

Lucas nodded, removing his jacket. 'I'll need to take a look at the notes.'

They'd fallen so easily into the familiar pattern. Lucas in the lead, studying Derek's notes and issuing instructions. Thea liaising with the ward sister and overseeing preparations. With two years' seniority to her, that had always been the way of it.

That had been the way of it seven years ago. Now this was *her* hospital. *Her* patient.

'You'll be sitting in on this one, then?' She murmured the question quietly.

For a moment he seemed lost for an answer. 'You've done this procedure before?'

What did he think she'd been doing for the last seven years? Lucas badly needed to catch up. 'Yes, many times.' She kept her voice low and professional, the barb in her words and not her tone. 'Some of them in conditions you could barely imagine.'

She might just as well have slapped him. The sting hit home and for a moment she saw hurt in his eyes. 'This is not about scoring points, Thea. It's about patient welfare.'

'So you're in the habit of questioning the competence of the doctors you work with?' Seven years ago she would have screamed the words at him. Now they were uttered quietly, between clenched teeth.

'Okay, I get it. This is *your* hospital...' His lip curled slightly.

'What the hell happened to you, Lucas?' Thea flushed red as she whispered the words. It might be inappropriate, but so what? The question had been on her mind ever since she'd first laid eyes on him yesterday.

'I got real.' He almost spat the words at her and then the consummate professional took over. 'I will sit in if that's okay with you.'

'Of course.' She turned on her heel and made her way back to Derek's room to take a breath and oversee the preparations. Anger had no place here, and neither did personal issues between doctors. What mattered was the patient, and that her hand was sure and steady.

A nurse helped Derek into position, leaning forward, and offering encouragement and a hand to hold. Thea concentrated on her job, the precise insertion of a needle into Derek's back in the spot indicated by the ultrasound scan. Fluid bubbled out from the pleural cavity, draining into a bag.

When it was done, a restrained burst of activity got Derek back comfortably into bed, and the room was cleared of the evidence of the procedure. Thea risked a glance in Lucas's direction, and he gave her a small nod of approval. She shouldn't need his acknowledgement, she knew for herself that everything had gone well. Maybe she'd just wanted it.

They were both treading on eggshells. Outwardly professional and confident but engaged in a private battle that had nothing to do with now and everything to do with their shared past. Lucas quirked his lips downwards. It wasn't really the shared past that was the problem. It was the things they hadn't shared, in the long years since he'd left her, that seemed to be the issue.

They were ready to leave the ward when a woman arrived. She looked tired, her dark hair scraped into a lank ponytail at the back of her head. Thea smiled, beckoning Lucas to follow her over.

'Anna. This is Dr West, he's working with me on Derek's case.'

Anna gave Lucas a cursory nod. 'How is Derek?'

'He's looking forward to seeing you. We did a procedure to drain the fluid from around his lungs this morning, and he should be much more comfortable now. Can we have a quick word with you?'

Somehow she managed to intimate that Lucas should follow them into the small area set aside for patients' families, without actually looking at him. He wondered whether he should offer to fetch coffee and decided against it. As Thea was so keen that this was *her* hospital, she would be the one to know where the coffee machine was.

'How's it going, Anna? Did you get some sleep last night?' Thea had sat down next to Anna and Lucas found a chair opposite them.

'A bit. Actually, it's almost a relief to know what's wrong with him after all this time. I know it's going to be difficult, but...'

'You'll have plenty of support, for as long as you need it.' Thea turned her lovely eyes onto him and suddenly everything else melted away. 'That's where Dr West comes in.'

Anna turned her expectant gaze onto Lucas. 'Yes?'

Lucas dragged his attention away from Thea and smiled at Anna. 'Part of my job is to provide clear information and advice about tuberculosis. If you have any questions, you can ask the doctors here, or you can ask me.'

Anna took the printed card that he proffered, stowing it in her handbag. 'Derek's a teacher, you know. And he's in a theatre group. But the last time he was there was before Christmas, when he painted the scenery for the pantomime. That was before he was ill.'

Anna was beginning to babble, and Lucas leaned forward to catch her attention. 'It's okay, Anna. We'll go through all the people he's been in contact with later.'

'It's just that I'm dreading what's going to happen when everyone finds out about this.'

'We realise that you're in a difficult situation.' He glanced at Thea, wondering if she felt that reassurance was her territory as well, but she simply nodded in agreement with him.

'We put a lot of effort into making the community aware of the facts. And one of those facts is that tuberculosis is not easily transmitted from one person to another.'

Anna rolled her eyes, giving him a watery smile. 'I understand that now. All the same, it feels as if it's all around me. And my children…'

'I saw in the notes that you have two children under five. And that they've both had their BCG.'

'That's right. I can't help worrying, though. I bleached everything last night.' Anna shivered, her gaze slewing around the room as if something was following her, waiting its chance to strike.

Giving her a leaflet wasn't going to do it.

'I understand that, but you were probably wasting your time.' Lucas shrugged. 'Apart from working off a bit of steam?'

Anna chuckled, her shoulders relaxing slightly. 'Yeah. I did that all right.'

'Well, that's something. Did you open the windows?'

'No, I…'

Anna didn't need to explain. Lucas had seen enough people instinctively shutting themselves in their houses, out of nameless fear. 'Well, that's what you need to do. Tuberculosis is transmitted aerobically and not via surfaces. Sunshine and fresh air are the best ways to eradicate the infection.'

Anna gave a snort of wry amusement. 'That's a nice thought.'

'It happens to be scientifically true. But you're quite at liberty to draw any metaphors you like from it.' Both women were smiling now, and Lucas felt like a showman. One with a serious intent, who nonetheless got a buzz out of delighting his audience.

'Okay. Now that Dr West has shed a little light on things…' Thea paused to grimace at her own, truly dreadful, pun. 'Dr West is going to be asking you about all the people who've been in close contact. I explained that to you yesterday.'

Anna nodded. 'Yes. I want to help.'

Lucas nodded his thanks. 'Why don't you go and see Derek now, and I'll come and find you in an hour? We'll chat then, over a cup of coffee.' He could find the machine. And if Thea wanted to join them, he'd get coffee for her as well.

The doors of the isolation unit clicked closed behind them. Lucas was strolling beside her, his jacket slung over one shoulder. 'We're agreed, then. You get to do the real work and leave the bureaucracy to me.' He was grinning.

'I didn't say that.' Thea attempted a severe look and failed. After all he'd done to assuage Anna's fears it wasn't easy to be angry with him.

'My mistake. I could have sworn that was the general drift of it.'

She gave an exaggerated shrug. 'Maybe I…'

'Overreacted?' He gave her a devastating smile.

'Probably.' She'd give him that. Asking him what the hell had happened to him hadn't been entirely necessary.

'Then you'll admit that I haven't gone over to the dark side.'

'Don't push it, Lucas. Anyway, there *is* no dark side.' She couldn't pretend that she hadn't thought it. And Lucas had always been able to read her like a book.

'Thank you.' He gave her a self-satisfied smirk. 'I'll take that as a yes.'

CHAPTER THREE

Week Two

THE WEEK HAD flown by in a blur of activity. Lucas had visited the school where Derek Thompson taught, and had collected information from both Anna and Derek. The theatre group had been investigated, but since Derek had been asymptomatic for some months after he'd last seen any of its members, they were deemed to be at no risk of infection.

By the following Monday they had finalised a set of standard letters, along with lists of people to whom each should be sent. And Thea had convinced herself that there would be no more petty arguments between her and Lucas.

She had no reason to take him up on his assurances that he would be there if needed until the Friday evening, almost two weeks after the initial diagnosis of TB had been made. Dialling his mobile number, she wondered what she might hear in the background.

'Thea. What's the problem?'

That just about said it all. He knew she wouldn't call him unless she had to.

'There's something I'd like to talk through with you. I've had a call from the local paper. I reckoned that was more your area of expertise than mine.'

Thea's one horrific contact with the press in Bangladesh had taught her to avoid newsmen at all costs. Lucas's world of measured responses and careful PR was far better equipped to deal with that than she was.

'Right.' A note of resignation sounded in his voice. 'What did they have to say for themselves?'

'They've been contacted by one of the parents at the school. They're doing a piece and they offered us the chance to comment. And they need our response by tomorrow afternoon, before they go to press.'

He gave a short chuckle. 'Nice one. Clearly hoping we'll be uncontactable at the weekend.'

'They do that sort of thing?'

'It's not unknown. I think we'll be pleased to respond. Do you have a copy of the proposed article?'

'No.' Thea supposed she should have thought to ask for one but she'd wanted to get the reporter off the phone as quickly as possible.

'Okay, give me their number and I'll call them now. Can we meet up this evening to discuss this?'

'I'll wait here for you. How long will you be?'

'I can't get there tonight. But I'm only twenty minutes away from you, and Friday night is barbecue night. Come and join us.'

Us. It had crossed Thea's mind that Lucas might be married, and she'd decided that was none of her concern. All the same, she wasn't sure that she wanted to play happy families with him.

'What about tomorrow morning? I don't want to interrupt your evening.'

'I'm working anyway. And there's an old acquaintance I'd like you to meet.'

'Who?' He'd married someone she knew? Thea *really* didn't want to know now.

'You'll see. I'll text my address. Dinner's in an hour.'

'But… Lucas?' She glared at the phone. He'd rung off.

It would serve him right if she just didn't turn up. She could text him the reporter's mobile number and leave him to deal with it. But not turning up might look as if she cared. Her phone beeped, and she looked at the screen.

She couldn't remember the number, but this was the road his parents had lived in. Large houses set well back from the road behind iron railings. The kind of place that simply screamed money and respectability. Lucas had loved his family but had always claimed he wanted a different way of life.

Numbness settled over her. If he could look her in the eye, when he'd trashed all the values and ideals that had meant so much to him, then he really wasn't the person she'd once known. If he could pretend that it didn't matter, he was nothing to her.

She texted back her reply, together with the contact number for the newspaper reporter. Then she grabbed her coat and bag and made for the hospital car park.

The house was easy to find. It had to be the smallest in the road but it was still imposing enough, and stood next to the house that Thea had been to when she and Lucas had visited his parents. Travelling the world, eh? He hadn't gone very far.

Even the dividing fence between his house and his parents' had been taken out, one drive serving both properties now. Thea parked in the space next to Lucas's car and took a moment to steady herself.

Climbing plants wound around the Victorian-style portico of his front door, and instead of a bell there was a heavy brass knocker in the shape of a dolphin. Almost as soon as she knocked on the door, it opened.

A teenage girl answered. Dark-eyed, with dark hair, she looked suspiciously like Lucas, but none of the sums added up. The girl was definitely a good bit more than seven years old. The thought that Lucas had been even more of a fraud that she'd bargained for floated into Thea's mind.

'Thea?' The girl grinned at her as if she knew her. 'Come in.'

She stepped into a large hallway and the girl closed the front door behind her. 'You don't know who I am, do you? I'm Ava.'

'Lucas's niece?' The last time she'd seen Ava she had been six years old, and they'd played football together in the back garden while Lucas and his brother had argued about medical aid in the developing world.

'Yes.' When Ava smiled, she looked even more like Lucas. 'I suppose I have changed a bit.'

'It's so nice to see you, Ava.' It was such a relief to see her. Unless Lucas had another surprise hostess tucked up his sleeve somewhere. 'You're staying with your uncle?'

'I live here.' Ava wheeled around with impetuous energy. 'I'll show you around.'

'Thank you. Where's Lucas?'

'Out back, lighting the barbecue. I'd stay clear if I were you. I always do.' Ava danced back towards Thea, leaning in close as if she had a secret to impart. 'He's not very good at it.'

'Which naturally makes him cross.' Lucas never had liked being outmatched by anything.

'Yep. He gets over it. When we see smoke signals coming over the horizon, it'll be safe to come out of hiding.' Ava opened one of the doors leading from the hallway. 'Sitting room.'

Thea peered past Ava into the comfortable, bright sitting room. 'Very nice.'

'Dining room…' Ava was on to the next room before Thea had a chance to even cross the threshold of the first.

'Equally nice.' Thea grinned at her.

'Kitchen…' Another door, which revealed a gleaming kitchen. 'We won't go in there.'

'Very wise. Leave the cooking to Lucas.'

'Do you remember when we roasted chestnuts in the fire

on Bonfire Night?' Ava didn't stop for an answer. 'Would you like to see my room?'

'I'd love to. If you'd like to show it to me.' Thea draped her coat over the banisters and put her heavy bag down in the corner. She felt suddenly lighter as she followed Ava up the stairs and into a large, stylishly decorated room.

'I went on holiday with Gran and Grandpa, and when I got back Lucas had decorated it as a surprise. What do you think?'

'It's beautiful. He did all this?'

Ava nodded. 'Yes. He said that I needed something a bit different now that I'm older. I think it's turned out pretty well.'

'It's very sophisticated. I like the curtains.' A bold, confident pattern of yellow, purple and green, the shades somehow blending perfectly together.

'It's an old fifties print. We went up to town to look at some fabrics. Lucas said it was for the conservatory.'

'And you fell for it.' Thea grinned.

'He's good with surprises, he never lets on.'

'No, he doesn't, does he?' The time that Lucas had started driving, saying that they were going out for a pub lunch, and hadn't stopped until they'd reached the ferry for France. When they'd reached dry land again they'd driven all night and watched the sun come up over the bright, glittering waters of the Mediterranean.

That was the old Lucas. The one who would have taken such delight in planning a surprise like this. The one that Thea had told herself was lost for ever.

Ava was gazing down, out of the window, and opened it in response to something below. Lucas's voice floated upwards, along with a puff of charcoal smoke.

'Are you listening for the door, Ava?'

'Yes.' Ava shut the window again abruptly and Thea suppressed a smile. What was it Lucas used to say? If you want the right answers, you have to ask the right questions.

Maybe she should take that advice too. But if she wanted to know why Ava was living here and not with her parents, she should either wait for Ava to volunteer the information or ask Lucas.

'That's a great place to work.' She pointed to the desk, which sat in deep bay window on the far side of the room.

'Yeah. I think that was a hint.' Ava grinned wryly.

'Exams next year?' Thea couldn't remember whether Ava was fourteen or fifteen now.

'No, two years. I'm choosing my GCSE subjects now.'

She must be fourteen, then. 'What do you want to do?'

'History. I'm not sure about the rest, yet. I want to be an archaeologist.'

'That sounds great.'

'I've already been on a dig—last summer. They didn't let us do much on our own, but it was pretty cool.' Ava's eyes lit up with enthusiasm. 'Look.'

She grabbed Thea's hand and led her over to the desk. Inside the alcove, a pinboard was fixed to the wall, covered in photographs. 'That's Lucas and me, with my find.'

Lucas had his arm around Ava's shoulders and they were both pulling faces for the camera. Suddenly, seven years seemed like nothing. His hair looked as if it had been styled by the wind, and he was wearing a rock-band T-shirt that had seen better days. Longing reached into her stomach, gripped hard and then twisted.

'That's fabulous.'

'Isn't it? It's Samian ware. That's high-quality pottery from Italy or France that the Romans used to use.'

Thea dragged her eyes from Lucas's face and focussed on the piece of broken pottery that Ava was holding up. 'How interesting.'

'Yeah. That piece of pottery came from something like that.' Ava indicated a museum postcard of a glossy red bowl, with moulding around the base, pinned next to the photograph. 'I saw it in one of the side trenches, where the settlement put all their rubbish, and they let me pick it up after it was photographed. I was the first person to touch it since it got thrown there. Can you imagine that?'

All that Thea could imagine at the moment was Lucas. 'It must have been an amazing feeling.' The board was like a memory board. Ava as she remembered her, a six-year-old with her parents. Then, growing up, with Lucas. Something must have happened and Thea dreaded to ask what that might have been.

'There's one of you here somewhere.' Ava scanned the board and pointed to one at the top. Some older photos of Lucas, and in one of them he was sitting outside a tent, his arm around Thea.

'Ah! I remember that. We were at Glastonbury.' She'd looked so different then. It wasn't just the hair or the clothes, she'd looked carefree. Thea wondered if Lucas found her as changed as she did him.

'What did you do there? Lucas says you danced all night.'

Not all night. Thea and Lucas had loved to dance, but there had been another pastime that they'd loved even more. Alone in their tent, however many people were passing by outside and despite the lumps in the ground under her back. Or his.

'Yes, we danced all night. Got pretty muddy and didn't have any pieces of Samian pottery to show for it.'

Ava's laugh was cut short by footsteps on the stairs. When Lucas appeared in the doorway it was as if time had rolled back, catapulting her into the place where she loved him. Maybe it was the photographs on Ava's board. Maybe because of the way he was dressed. Jeans that fitted him like a glove and a rugby shirt that emphasised his broad shoulders so much better than a jacket and tie.

He threw Ava a reproachful look, which melted into the warmth that had been missing from his face over the last two weeks. 'Do you ladies want to eat tonight?'

'You want me to lay the table?' That was obviously Ava's job.

'I've already done it. Perhaps you'd like to get Thea a drink?'

'Oh. Yes. We were just talking about Glastonbury. She's told me all your secrets…' Ava continued provocatively.

'All of them?' A flicker at the side of one eye as his gaze met Thea's.

'Every one of them. How we danced all night.' That was all Ava needed to know, and anyway it wasn't her place to give away Lucas's secrets. Suddenly it mattered a great deal that there were things that only she and Lucas shared, that only they remembered.

He gave her an almost imperceptible nod and then an exaggerated shrug for Ava's benefit. 'Guess I've been rumbled, then. What do you want me to agree to this time?'

'Nothing yet. I'm storing it up for use later.' Ava shot him a grin and Lucas laughed, putting his arm around her shoulder.

'Okay. I'll consider myself warned. Now, hurry up, or dinner's going to be burned to a crisp.'

'She seems like a handful.' They'd eaten and Ava had disappeared into the house. Lucas tilted the half-empty bottle of wine towards Thea and she shook her head. 'No more, thanks. I'm driving.'

'She keeps me on my toes. Most difficult thing I've ever done. Most rewarding thing I've ever done.' He propped his feet up on the empty chair opposite him, leaning back to catch the evening sun.

'You've done a great job. How long has she lived with you?'

'Since she was seven. Her parents were killed in a car crash.'

Thea had steeled herself to hear something like that, but

it was still a shock. 'I'm sorry, Lucas. I liked your brother and his wife very much.'

'Yeah.' He ran his finger thoughtfully around the rim of his glass. 'They were good people.'

'When did it happen?'

'They were killed four days before I was due to leave for Bangladesh. We were all at my parents' house, for some family time before I went away, and they'd gone out to run some errands. Left Ava behind with me.' His voice was flat, matter-of-fact. 'I had to tell Ava that her mother and father weren't coming back, my mother couldn't do it.'

'That must have been terribly hard for you.'

'All I could think about was her. I promised her then that I'd look after her, and I have. My mother and father talked about adopting her, but then my mother was diagnosed with breast cancer. So I adopted Ava and Mum concentrated on getting well.'

'She's okay now?'

'Yeah, she's been clear for four years now. Ava's home is with me, but she spends a lot of time with my parents. It seems to work.'

He still hadn't answered the most important question. 'And what about you?'

'Me?' He put his hand on his chest, as if to check that he was really the object of her concern. 'What about me?'

He'd lost his brother and sister-in-law. His mother had been seriously ill, and he'd given up his own dreams to take on the challenge of caring for a grieving six-year-old. 'It was a lot for you to deal with as well.'

Lucas shook his head. 'Not as much as Ava or my mother. They were the ones…' His words tailed off into a remembrance of grief.

'You always seemed to want to go to Bangladesh so much.'

'I did, once upon a time.' Did he class his time with her

like that too? A distant fairy story, which had no bearing on reality?

'But not now?'

He turned to look at her, his gaze searching her face. 'No, not now. We all have dreams, and then we grow out of them.'

They were almost the hardest words she'd heard tonight. 'Is that why you asked me here? To meet Ava?'

'You rang me.' He seemed to relax the tight grip he had on his emotions a little. 'I'm glad you came. Ava remembers you and she's been wanting to see you again.'

No mention of his own feelings. It was as if the tragedy of losing his brother and the sudden responsibility of a child had quenched the passion that had so defined Lucas. Seeing him so changed... It would almost have been better never to have seen him at all.

'It's been good to be here.'

There was something he needed to get out of the way. Lucas told himself that it was all about their professional relationship and nothing about the personal. 'I wouldn't have blamed you if you'd refused to work with me. After the way that I left.'

'I always knew what you wanted to do. I supported you in that.' She shrugged, as if it really didn't matter.

He'd had time to reflect on the mistake he'd made in breaking up with her, and he knew now that it did matter. 'I called you. Before the funeral. I couldn't get through on your mobile and I didn't want to leave a message. So I tried the house you used to share.'

'What did they say?'

'That you'd gone abroad. That you wouldn't want to speak to me.'

She took a deep breath and a gulp of her wine.

'I didn't blame you, Thea. I'd half expected you to refuse to speak to me.'

She shook her head. 'That was… I got drunk one night and said it to the girls I lived with. I didn't mean it. Of course I would have spoken to you.'

'Where did you go?' Suddenly it was important that he knew.

Her gaze was on his face now and her cheeks were starting to burn red. 'I went to Bangladesh. It was my last summer before I started work and I thought it would be nice to drop in and see where you were staying. For a bit of a holiday…'

It was all falling into place. An exquisitely timed tragedy. He had left Thea, planning to spend a fortnight with his family before going to Bangladesh. And in that fortnight everything had changed. Sam and Claire had died. And however casual she made it sound, there was no doubt in his mind that Thea had decided to go to Bangladesh to find him.

'I'm sorry I missed you.'

'It wasn't your fault. I'm just sorry that I never knew about Sam and Claire.'

He didn't deserve her forgiveness, but he couldn't find a way to tell her that. It was almost a relief when she reached briskly for the pile of papers that she'd propped on the windowsill behind her.

'Thanks for tonight, but I'm really tired. Could I call you tomorrow morning to discuss our reply to the newspaper article?'

That would be good. There were far too many questions swimming in his head at the moment to concentrate on anything. 'Yes, of course. I'll be around all morning.'

Thea felt sick. She stopped the car, wondering whether it would be better to reach for the empty shopping bag under the seat, stick her fingers down her throat and get it over with.

Probably not. The feeling was in her chest and nothing to do with her stomach.

He'd had good reasons for not being on that plane. He'd called her. If she'd known either of those things, what had happened next might have been very different. Instead, she'd been too proud to contact Lucas and had continued on a path that would lead to disgrace.

She switched on the car radio and then thought better of it, punching the 'off' button. The radio had turned into something like a game of Russian roulette, never knowing whether the next track would be the one which reminded her of Lucas.

Just drive. Go home. Get some sleep. She had put her life back together again, piece by piece, but Thea knew that it was still a shaky structure. And Lucas had already broken her heart once. Long and slow, bit by bit, from the moment he'd left her to the time she'd realised he wasn't in Bangladesh. If she was going to keep it all together now, she had to somehow stop caring about him.

CHAPTER FOUR

Week Three

SHE LOOKED LOVELY, almost like the young woman he'd once known. Apart from her hair, and Lucas was getting used to that and actually thought it rather suited her. It was just that he remembered when it had tumbled down her back. When he'd let it slide through his fingers. The night she'd lain on her back while he'd brushed it out in a shining circle around her head. It had been as if they'd been making love on golden sheets.

No more fairy tales. Thea was more like a pageboy than a princess now, seeming to go out of her way to be inconspicuous. A ferocious, committed pageboy, and today a rather glamorous one, who wore a neat, dark jacket and skirt instead of her usual trousers. Her gleaming hair was brushed in a don't-mess-with-me arrangement and she had a little make-up on. Small changes that were killing Lucas, because at this moment all he wanted to do was mess with her.

The press conference was at two that afternoon, and Thea had disappeared just when he wanted to do a final run-through of the answers to all the expected questions. No one in the department had seen her, she wasn't in the canteen, and the incident team's office was empty.

Not quite empty. There was no answer when he called

her name but a rustle and the sound of laboured breathing
from behind a door in the corner told him that someone
was there. Lucas didn't think he'd ever actually opened
that door, reckoning that it was probably a cupboard of
some sort.

It was. A large store cupboard, intended to hold the medical supplies for the adjoining clinic. When Lucas opened
the door, Thea was perched precariously on the windowsill, breathing into a paper bag.

'Thea?' He advanced towards her and she almost shrank
from him, her breath coming faster now. Lucas stopped,
three feet away from her. 'Are you all right?'

Of course she wasn't. Her breathing was fast and ir-
regular, overfilling her lungs with oxygen. The paper bag
didn't seem to be helping at all, because she could hardly
hold it to her lips.

She couldn't speak but she motioned him away angrily,
as if it was his fault that he'd seen the weakness behind her
veneer. Lucas put the sheaf of papers he was carrying onto
one of the shelves that lined the wall and walked slowly
towards her. Even that seemed to spook her.

'Can you walk?'

She ignored him completely. Even if she could walk,
she obviously wasn't intending to go anywhere with him.
Lucas turned and flipped the lock on the door, wondering
how incriminating it would look if anyone found them
locked in a store cupboard together. As long as her boss
didn't hear of it, he was probably in the clear.

'You're all right.' He held the crumpled paper bag to her
lips. 'Just breathe.'

Her eyes were wild, the way he'd used to love them,
but she did what he asked. Lucas counted out the breaths,
his hand light on her back as reassurance, and slowly she
began to calm.

'Would you like some water?'

She just looked at him so Lucas fetched the bottle of

water he'd been carrying with his papers. Held it to her lips and she sipped a little, gratefully.

'What's going on, Thea?' Once upon a time she would've told him. Things were different now.

'I'm okay. Just a little tired.'

'Yeah. Pull the other one.' He said the words gently. 'Tired doesn't give you panic attacks.'

'I just need a minute. Don't fuss.'

So that was how she intended to play it. As a doctor, there was little more that Lucas could do, and he had no intention of rekindling their relationship. Nothing said they couldn't be friends, though. He sat down beside her on the windowsill, put his arm around her shoulders and gave her a hug.

He felt her stiffen and then relax. Lucas had thought he remembered how good her body felt against his, but he hadn't. It was almost impossible to hold her without kissing her.

His lips formed the shape of a kiss into the air above her head. A fragile thing that died as soon as it was born, instead of leading into a smile and then something delicious. Lucas held her for a few moments more and then gently drew back.

'Are you going to tell me what's going on?'

She shook her head. 'No.'

'Okay, then. Keep it to yourself.'

That got the ghost of a smile from her. 'We should make a move. You don't want to be late for your public.'

'You need to rest.'

'I do not.'

'Have it your own way. I'm not taking you into a press conference wondering if you'll be whipping out a paper bag to breathe into any moment. It's not the most reassuring look.'

'You don't need to wonder. I've had my moment.'

She seemed steady enough now, if a little washed out. Lucas got to his feet. 'Stay here. I'll handle it.'

'We agreed that you and someone from the hospital should attend. Provide a cohesive response.'

'Michael Freeman's here. I'll ask him to stand in.'

A look of alarm crossed her face and he sat down again, wondering if he was going to need the paper bag again.

'You will not. This is *my* job.'

'Something to prove?'

'Yes, of course I do. Don't tell me that you're any different.'

Thea wasn't fearless, never had been. Only those with no understanding of the consequences of a situation were completely without fear. But this was the response she'd always given to things that frightened her. She faced them, just to show who was boss.

'I need to know, then.'

She shrugged. 'I don't much like the idea of sitting in front of a crowd of people and being photographed. I've never been at a press conference before.'

'Well, it's not much like TV. No shouting and flashing bulbs, they're usually quite civilised.' He grinned. 'The ones I give are, anyway.'

'That's a relief.'

He chanced another question. 'I hope you didn't mind that I let Ava have your photograph to put on her board.'

For a moment she truly didn't see the connection, and then understanding dawned on her face. 'Of course not. It was nice to see it again.'

He nodded. 'So you don't mind old photos—just new ones.'

She looked at him with that blank expression that signalled something she didn't want to talk about. 'Something like that.'

'Okay. I'll figure it out.'

Half the puzzle had fallen into place, leaving the other

half even more tantalisingly unknown than before. Every-thing that Thea did now seemed focussed on not drawing too much attention to herself. All he needed to know now was why that was so important to her.

'Look, let's just go and get this done.' The old Thea sur-faced suddenly. The one who didn't let anything get in her way, not even him. If she had the assembled newsmen as firmly under her spell as she did him, they'd have nothing to worry about.

'Wait a minute...' He walked to the door, listening to make sure that no one was outside. He didn't have a plan for what he might do if he heard anything.

She slid past him and opened the door, to reveal an empty office. 'I don't imagine anyone's got a problem with our inspecting the stockroom, have they?'

He followed her outside, grinning. 'No. I don't imagine they have.'

Thea braved it out. She didn't feel all that brave and she was embarrassed that Lucas had found her having a panic at-tack in a cupboard, but he seemed to take that in his stride. He didn't leave her side, ushering her to her seat and sitting down next to her. His bulk, the way he naturally drew ev-eryone's attention and seemed to absorb it with ease, was reassuring. She could do this. There would be no repeat of Bangladesh, no shouting, no name-calling. This was just a group of men and women, with notepads and voice record-ers, who asked all the expected questions.

'Splendid!' Michael Freeman was smiling as they left their seats and the crowd in the room started to mingle. 'I thought that went very well.'

'Thanks.'

'You showed a collaborative working relationship, with everyone in agreement as to the best way to proceed.' Michael fixed her with a questioning look.

'That's how it is, Michael.'

'You'd tell me if it wasn't.'

'Of course. This is too important—' Thea broke off as a reporter with a camera appeared right in front of them.

'Can I have a picture?'

'Delighted. You're from…?' Suddenly Lucas was there, and it seemed that the camera was no longer pointing her way. Thea realised that she'd instinctively taken a few steps back, shrinking from the lens, and that Lucas had put himself in between her and the cameraman.

'The local paper. You commented on our article.'

'Ah, yes. I thought that was going to print over the weekend.' Lucas's smile took on a hint of confrontational charm.

'We held it until today, so that we could include what's been said at the press conference. In the interests of fairness.'

'That's good to hear.' Lucas shot a quick look in her direction and started to steer the cameraman away from her. 'Michael, perhaps you'd like to be in on this one?'

Michael raised his eyebrows but followed dutifully, leaving Thea to make her escape before anyone else could catch her. It would be a while before anyone noticed she'd gone and by then she'd be up on the ward and away from the circus of curious eyes and jutting lenses.

CHAPTER FIVE

Week Four

THEA SURVEYED THE empty waiting room. Three TB nurses had been working at full tilt all day to keep the numbers in the waiting room down, but it hadn't been easy. There were forms to be filled out, questions from worried parents and real and imagined symptoms to be investigated and advised on.

Lucas had seemed to expect all this, and was standing by to help when the flood of people wanting a doctor's advice had threatened to overwhelm Thea. He was relaxed and cheerful, his sleeves rolled up in a certain indication that he meant business, his demeanour inviting the world in general to tell him what was on its mind. She'd seen a new side to him today. Passion, tempered by professionalism.

'That's everyone?' He gave a farewell nod to a woman who'd gone into his consulting room looking as if she was on her way to a funeral and come out again looking as if she was vaguely considering going to a party.

'That's it. You were a long time with that last patient.' Everyone else had packed up and gone home, leaving Thea to try and make some inroads into the pile of paperwork on her desk.

'She was telling me all about the new leisure centre

that's been built just down the road. Apparently they've
got a dance studio down there with a proper sprung floor.'

'Really? They do classes?'

'Yeah, apparently. Thinking of going?'

For a moment his smile tempted her and Thea considered the prospect. She hadn't danced for ages, and suddenly
she missed it. But she had no partner.

'I don't have the time these days.' Thea picked up her
pen and then threw it back down again, deciding that she'd
get through the stack of files much quicker if she took them
home with her and had something to eat first. 'Besides, I'd
rather take a course that's more practical. Something like
self-defence maybe.'

'You're worried about your safety?'

Thea ignored the question. She really didn't want to
get into that.

Lucas shrugged, and let it go. 'Would you like a lift?
I've got my car with me today.'

She couldn't think of a good reason to say no. Other
than the truth, and it wasn't for him to know that she was
enjoying working with him far more than she should. Thea
returned his smile. 'Okay, yes. I could do with a lift tonight, I'm tired.'

They locked the door of the clinic and walked to the car
park. 'If you find a good self-defence class, let me know.
I might suggest it to Ava.'

'Okay. Ava and I could go together perhaps.'

'I think she'd like that. I'm all for it.'

He drove slowly towards the hospital gates, stopping
to let an ambulance through to the forecourt of the A and
E department. As he stopped again to let someone run
across the crossing in front of him, the screech of brakes
and a dull thud sounded from somewhere. Something right
at the periphery of her vision, moving fast, made Thea
instinctively shrink back in her seat, one hand flying up
to shield her face.

The engine shrieked in protest as Lucas changed gear and reversed, fast. A large chunk of metal hit the road a few feet in front of the car, just about where Thea had been sitting a few seconds ago. There was a moment of silence and then the sound of someone shouting.

'You all right?' Lucas had instinctively flung one arm protectively across her.

'Yes. Are you?'

'Yeah.'

He wrenched his door open, and Thea followed suit, practically tumbling out of the car. An ambulance had been turning right into the hospital, across a lane of traffic, and it looked as if it had been hit by a car coming the other way. Its side had been stoved in, and the impact had pushed it out of control and into one of the brick pillars that supported the gates.

People were running. A group of nurses who had been chatting and laughing together, off duty for the night, had dropped their bags and coats and were legging it across the road towards a silver car, which had spun across two lanes of traffic and crashed into someone's front wall. Lucas sprinted past her and Thea followed him.

'The ambulance driver...' he called to her, before making his way around to the back of the vehicle. There was a doctor already running to the car, and Thea opened the driver's door of the ambulance.

'Are you all right?' The driver seemed dazed, but she had been held firmly in her seat by her seat belt and protected by the air bag.

'Think so. He came out of nowhere...' The young woman suddenly snapped back into coherence, and she twisted around to look through the glass into the back of the ambulance. 'Dave? My partner's in the back.'

And he would have been sitting right where the ambulance had taken the most impact. 'There's someone back there already.' Thea leaned over and released the woman's seat belt. 'What's your name?'

'Lisa. I'm okay, you don't need to go through all that with me.'

'Indulge me.' Thea helped Lisa down from the cabin and walked her to a bench by the hospital gates. 'Sit.'

Lisa rolled her eyes but did it anyway. Thea beckoned to a nurse who had just arrived to help and left her trying to keep Lisa under control while she hurried to the back of the ambulance.

Lucas was struggling with the doors, which had been bent out of alignment by the impact. She could hear someone crying for help now from inside. One great heave, accompanied by a roar of effort, and the doors opened and Lucas levered himself upwards into the back of the ambulance.

Inside, a man was sitting upright on a carry chair, still secured in place by the straps across his body. On the other side, where the impact had been, it was a different story. The wall of the ambulance was twisted and buckled, and a man in uniform, who had to be Lisa's partner Dave, was lying on the floor. In the silence, the beep of a monitor sounded loudly.

'Help him. Please, help him...' The man on the chair was conscious and seemed lucid, more worried about the crew who had brought him here than himself. Thea scrambled up into the ambulance to get a better view, as Lucas quickly checked Dave out. He wasn't breathing and already going into cyanosis. Blood covered his face and the front of his shirt, and his jaw was obviously broken.

'We won't get a line in to intubate. You've done a temporary crike before?' Lucas looked up at her.

'Yep.' A cricothyroidotomy was easier to do than a full tracheotomy in an emergency situation, and the results were more reliable. This close to the hospital, the question of how long it would remain stable was irrelevant.

Lucas had already located the kit and broken it open, half filling the cannula with sterile saline. Handing it to Thea, he moved Dave's head back.

Her hand shook. She'd done this before, but never with the thought that a whole hospital full of medical professionals would be assessing her every move the next morning. The sudden thought that she might fail, and what she'd say to them if she did, paralysed her.

'You're good to go, Thea.' Lucas's voice was calm.

Dave was going to die if she didn't do this. That was more important than anything that anyone could possibly say to her afterwards. She positioned one hand around Dave's neck, holding both sides of the airway, and slid the needle in. Bubbles rose into the body of the cannula, indicating that she'd found the airway.

She held the needle in place, while Lucas removed the syringe and attached the oxygen tube. After an agonising moment Dave's chest began to rise and fall.

'Looks as if there are some chest injuries as well.' Lucas glanced up at the paramedic who was outside the doors of the ambulance, talking to the other passenger, keeping his attention away from the lifesaving procedures that she and Lucas were undertaking. 'We need to get him out of here as soon as he's stable.'

'We'll be ready to move him in a few minutes,' the paramedic replied quickly and then turned his attention back to his charge. There seemed to be no lack of resources at this particular accident scene.

Lucas opened Dave's bloodied shirt, and she caught sight of a little gold St Christopher around his neck. She swallowed hard, pulling her gaze away, concentrating on the injuries she could see. Dave's breathing was fast and shallow, and his chest was rising and falling unevenly.

'Flail chest?' She nodded to the area that seemed to be moving in the opposite direction of everything else.

'Yep.' Lucas covered the area with a wad of dressing,

keeping his hand firmly over the area. Dave's breathing stabilised, and Lucas gave a grim smile of satisfaction. 'Is the gurney here yet?'

'We're ready.' A call came from outside, and Lucas acknowledged it with a nod.

'Okay. We need to do this carefully. You'll make sure the needle doesn't move?' His gaze met Thea's for a moment.

'Yes. You keep up the pressure on his chest. The guys will move him.'

The tricky business of getting Dave out from where he lay on the floor of the ambulance and onto a gurney was accomplished with the minimum of fuss. His colleagues carried him carefully to the entrance of the A and E department, Lucas walking on one side, keeping pressure on his chest, and Thea on the other.

Jake Turner was ready for them inside, ushering them to a cubicle. Thea waited patiently, concentrating on her part of the effort to keep Dave alive for long enough to get him to surgery. When her turn came to be relieved of her duties, her arms would hardly respond from the effort of keeping them in one place for so long.

'Okay, we're going to take him down now.' The beep of the monitor, assessing Dave's heart rate, was fast but reassuringly regular. Intravenous drips were already in place, and Jake had assessed all Dave's injuries. 'Good work, everyone.'

It had taken three quarters of an hour and seven people, all working together, to get Dave this far. They'd bought enough time to give the surgeons and the intensive care staff a chance to do their work.

'Okay?' Lucas had stripped his surgical gloves off and was washing the blood from his forearms, using the basin in the now-empty cubicle.

'Yeah.' Thea realised that she was trembling. 'Just a bit stiff.'

'I'm not surprised, the way you were bent over.' He

pulled a towel from the dispenser, leaving the tap running so that she could wash. 'You know him?'

'I've seen him around, that's all.' She heaved a sigh. 'He's one of us, though.'

'Yeah. Makes it harder. Knowing that everyone's going to have an opinion by tomorrow, whatever you do.'

She shivered. 'Don't.'

He was wiping his hands, looking at her thoughtfully. 'Doing something is the reason we became doctors.'

Thea had thought that in Bangladesh. She'd done something when no one else would, and had been condemned for it.

'Yeah.' She shook her head. This was an entirely different situation. Lucas had been there and he'd been with her all the way. And Dave was in surgery now, with a good chance of pulling through.

'Cup of tea?'

'I want to wait, see if there's any news.'

'That's what I thought. So we'll have a cup of tea while we do it.' A commotion from outside made Lucas's head jerk round and he strode to the door of the cubicle. As he opened it, Lisa's voice rose above the others'.

'How many times have I got to tell you? I'm all right. I'm going...'

One of the A and E nurses was trying to pacify her. 'You need to wait here until a doctor can see you. And everyone's busy right now.'

'Yeah, well, I've got somewhere I need to be right now. And I'm quite capable of working out if I have a concussion.'

'No, Lisa, you're not. I know you think you're okay, and you probably are, but you've just been in a major accident. If it was anyone else, you'd be the first to tell them that they needed to see a doctor.'

The nurse wasn't having much success. Lisa had turned

abruptly away from her and was about to walk away when
Lucas blocked her path.

'Hi. I happen to be a doctor.'

Thea supposed that she really should have done the examination herself, as she was employed by the hospital and
Lucas wasn't. But Lucas had exactly what Lisa needed
at the moment, an easy, joking manner and the ability to
make her see sense without ramming the regulations down
her throat.

'Wait…' He was working carefully and thoroughly, and
had got to the point of checking the reaction of Lisa's pupils to light. 'Don't look up until I tell you.'

'You were about to tell me.' Lucas and Lisa had been
battling their way through the whole examination.

'No, I wasn't.' He paused for about two seconds. 'Look
up, please.'

'Everyone loves a smart-arse.' Thea suppressed a smile
as Lisa took the words right out of her own mouth.

'Yeah, and everyone loves a patient who knows better
than they do.' Lucas chuckled.

'I've had a few of those in my time.'

'Yeah, I'll bet.' Lucas flipped off the penlight. 'Okay,
well, I'm disappointed to tell you that I can't find anything
wrong with you.'

Lisa slipped off the gurney, sliding her feet back into her
heavy boots. 'Sure you didn't miss anything?'

Lucas shrugged. 'I can try again, if you want.'

'Nah. Thanks, though. I've got to go and see what's
happening.'

'Dave's not going to be out of surgery for a while yet.'
Thea spoke quietly.

'Yeah, I know.' Lisa twisted her lips together.

'Why don't you have a cup of tea with us?' Lucas looked
around to see whether anyone was waiting for Lisa, but no
one seemed to be.

'I want to find out what happened.' Lisa's face took on a sullen look, and suddenly it hit Thea. She'd been busy worrying about whether her own actions would stand the test of scrutiny, and not even thought that Lisa had been driving when the accident had happened.

'Wait here, Lisa.' She rose from her seat.

'I'm going—' The argumentative tone sounded in Lisa's voice again.

'Sit. Down.' Both Thea and Lisa started, and Thea almost sat down, even though Lucas's words were directed at Lisa. She supposed that bringing up a teenager had honed the sudden command in his voice.

Lisa sat back down on the gurney.

'Stay there. If you don't do as you're told, I'll admit you.'

'What for?' One last trace of Lisa's defiance remained.

'I'll make something up. I don't suppose you have a cough?'

Lucas fetched a cup of tea for Lisa, keeping his eye on the cubicle door. Thea had bolted, obviously on a mission to get whatever information she could, and he wasn't about to let Lisa make a break for it in the meantime. Ten minutes later Thea returned, a grim smile on her face.

'Okay. There's no news on Dave yet, but there's something else...' She sat down next to Lisa on the gurney. 'The other driver was drunk. There were a couple of eyewitnesses, who both said they saw you turning into the hospital and that the other guy came round the corner and shot the lights, going straight into you. There was no way you could have seen him.'

Lisa stared at her for a moment, and then clapped her hand over her mouth, squeezing her eyes shut. 'Oh. Thank God.' She shook her head. 'No...I don't mean that...'

'I know what you meant.'

Lisa slumped against Thea, the tough exterior of an experienced ambulance driver suddenly dissolved. 'I thought it was my fault.'

Lucas just managed to hook a cardboard bowl from the pile and thrust it into Thea's hand before Lisa was sick. It was a short, sharp reaction, and Lucas got rid of the bowl while Thea looked after Lisa.

'Ugh.' Lisa took the paper towel that Thea proffered and wiped her mouth. 'Is the driver all right, then? The car looked as if it was a complete wreck.'

Somehow Lisa managed to carry off the combination of utter disgust for the driver of the car with concern for his well-being.

Thea grinned at her. 'Broken arm. Apart from that and being under arrest he's fine.'

'The police are here?'

'Yes. Keeping a low profile, but they breathalysed the guy and the last anyone saw of him was that an officer was following him round to X-Ray.' Thea slipped her arm around Lisa's shoulders. 'Come on. I'll help you clean up, and then we'll get a cup of tea. By that time there might be some news.'

By the time they got to the relatives' lounge Dave's wife was already there, accompanied by two men, still in uniform and obviously just off shift. Lisa faltered when she saw her and Thea squeezed her arm.

'Lisa! I've been worried about you.'

'Marie. I'm so sorry.'

'Don't be silly. It's not your fault.' Marie took Lisa in her arms, hugging her tight, and Thea saw a tear roll down Lisa's cheek. Someone brought a seat for her, and the two women sat together, Lisa's arm around Marie's shoulders.

Lucas waited with them until Dave got out of surgery. When a nurse came to collect Marie, saying she'd be allowed a few minutes with Dave, she insisted that Lisa

should go too, and the two women made their way to the
ICU together.

Thea didn't move as the group of work colleagues who'd
been waiting for news dispersed. Lucas was sitting, his
legs stretched out in front of him, showing no inclination
to do anything either.

'We must do this again some time.' He didn't speak
until they were alone.

'Yeah.' Thea knew what he meant. She always had with
Lucas.

'Not the serious injury part.'

'Clearly. Or the drunken driver part.' It was the realisation that even though they were both doctors, even though
they'd done practically everything else together, they'd
never done this. Never saved a man's life.

She could have just sat here with him all night, sharing
that quiet satisfaction. Instead, Thea got to her feet. 'Is that
lift home still on offer?'

'Yeah. Of course.'

CHAPTER SIX

THE WEEK DIDN'T let up on them. As soon as the Mantoux tests were all administered, there was the work of seeing everyone again to check the results. A hard, raised area at the site of the injection, which measured more than ten millimetres across, was classed as a reaction to the tuberculin test and required further investigation.

The results were good for most. But so far Thea and Lucas had seen two teachers and six pupils whose tests had been positive. Each was given a thorough examination to check whether there was any sign of active tuberculosis, and X-rays and blood tests were taken.

At three o'clock Thea took a moment for lunch at her desk. Which meant that she was looking straight at Lucas, whose desk had been pushed up against hers, directly opposite, to accommodate the growing team. She was just debating whether to concentrate on her sandwich or watch him work when the phone rang.

'I'll get it. Eat your lunch.' He reached across and hooked the receiver up with one finger. 'Lucas West.'

He listened intently and then nodded. 'Okay, we'll see her now.'

'I thought we were finished?' Thea laid her sandwich down on the napkin in front of her.

'It's the girl who didn't show up for her appointment. I got the team secretary to ring the school and apparently one of the teachers has found her and brought her down here. I suppose we'd better see her before she tries to make a break for it. Want me to go?'

'No, that's okay. Finish your notes. And don't touch my sandwich.'

'Right. Finish your sandwich. Don't touch my notes.'

'Yeah. Funny.'

When Thea entered the consulting room the girl swung round in her seat to face her. She looked much older than sixteen. Her blonde hair showed signs of dark roots and her school uniform had been adjusted, the skirt shorter and the tie knotted three inches lower than it was meant to be. Thea could identify with the tie at least. Whoever had thought it was a good idea to make sixteen-year-old girls wear ties to school was just as mistaken now as when she'd been that age.

'Isobel Grant?'

The girl's gaze was cool and calculating. 'Yes?'

'I'm Dr Coleman. Would you like your teacher to be here while I examine you?' Clearly Isobel's parents weren't here. It never failed to depress Thea that that wasn't particularly unusual.

Isobel pressed her lips together. 'No. I'm sixteen, I can make my own mind up about things.'

She knew the law, then. At sixteen she was considered competent to make medical decisions for herself. Even if she was little more than a child in some respects and a little parental support might have been nice.

Thea sat down on one of the chairs beside Isobel. 'You know why you've been tested?'

Isobel gave her a look of mild derision. 'Yes. And if the test swells up into a lump, I might have TB. But it hasn't.'

'Okay. I'm still going to need to see it, though.' Thea shrugged. 'Just to confirm.'

Isobel rolled up her sleeve. The area on her arm where the Mantoux test had been administered was red and sore

looking but there was no hard lump, indicating a reaction
to the tuberculin test.

'Good. That's very good. I'm happy to say that your test
is negative, Isobel. Just as you said.'

'Thanks. That's good.' Tears suddenly welled in Isobel's
eyes.

'Were you worried about the test?'

Isobel stared at her, wiping her face with the cuff of
her blazer.

'Do you have any other symptoms? A cough?'

'No.'

'Do you wake up in the night, sweating?'

'No. I never wake up in the night.'

'And you've not lost any weight recently?'

'No!' Thea jumped as Isobel shouted the word. 'There's
nothing. I'm okay. You said so, the test's negative.'

'Isobel, something's the matter. You didn't turn up for
your appointment this morning, and now you're crying.'

'It happens.' Isobel was rocking in her chair now, tears
running down her cheeks. Thea tried to put her arm around
her shoulders but Isobel batted her away.

Thea was at a loss. She'd done what she had to do and
Isobel's test was negative. But she couldn't let her go, not
while she was obviously so distressed. On the other hand,
if Isobel decided to leave, she couldn't think of a valid reason for stopping her.

A quiet knock sounded on the door. Thea called for whoever it was to come in, and Lucas's head appeared. 'Can I
speak to you a moment?'

'Yes.' Whatever it was he wanted, Thea was grateful
for the interruption. Time to think. 'Isobel, will you wait
here, please? Just one minute.'

'Anything the matter?' He waited until Thea had closed
the consulting-room door behind her. 'I heard shouting.'

'I don't know. Her test's negative, but she's very distressed. She won't say what's wrong, but I think it may be something to do with being tested.'

He pursed his lips. 'You want me to bring some tea for her?'

'I don't know. Maybe.'

'Would you like me to try her?'

Thea shrugged. 'Well, you can't do any worse than I've been doing so far.'

'I'll get some tea, then. Go and sit with her.'

Isobel didn't seem any more inclined to talk when Thea returned to the room, and she was still crying. Quietly and steadily, like a long wail of anguish. In Thea's experience, that kind of crying came from despair.

Five minutes later Lucas appeared, three cups of tea balanced in his hands. He sat down behind the desk, pushing two of the cups towards Thea and Isobel and keeping one for himself.

'Right. Isobel.'

Isobel looked at him mutely.

'I've brought you a cup of tea because we might need to wait here for a while.' Clearly Lucas reckoned that he could outlast Isobel. Maybe he could.

'I can't. I have to get home. I can't be late.' Isobel sniffled at him.

'All right. So we've got a problem. I reckon you can do with some help. I'd like to help you, but I can't unless you tell me how.'

'There's nothing you can do.' Isobel jutted her chin at him defiantly.

'Try me.' Lucas batted the challenge right back at her.

'It's nothing… I'm just…' Isobel heaved a sigh. 'My mum's ill. I was worried about my test because I didn't want to pass anything on to her.'

Thea exchanged a quick glance with Lucas. 'What's the matter with your mum, Isobel? Does she have a cough?'

Isobel rolled her eyes. 'No. She has cancer.'

'I'm sorry to hear that.' Thea bit her lip. So much for jumping to conclusions. There were enough kids in this area whose parents didn't care enough to accompany them to a hospital visit, but it seemed that Isobel wasn't one of them.

'If I had TB, then I'd have to stay away from her. She has a compromised immune system, due to the chemo. Then she'd have no one to look after her.'

'Is it just you and your mum?' Lucas asked.

'Yes. I can manage, we don't need anyone else.'

'It must be pretty hard for you, though.' His voice was calm, gentle, but Isobel burst into great racking sobs. When Thea put her arm around her shoulders, she clung to her, crying like a baby.

'She's okay?' When Thea walked back into the office an hour later, Lucas was sitting at his desk.

Thea shrugged. 'As well as can be expected, in the circumstances. I took her up to Maggie, the hospital social worker, and she's going to take her home. I think Isobel understands that we're not going to try and take her away from her mother, and she knows that there are some practical ways that we can help her.'

Lucas shook his head. 'She needs help. She's only sixteen, and trying to look after her mother and keep up with her schoolwork. It's too much, both physically and emotionally. Is that why she didn't say anything? Because she was afraid that she'd be taken into care?'

'Yeah. And she turned sixteen last week. So perhaps the thought that she was safe from that now, coupled with the worry over the Mantoux test, just pushed her over the edge.'

'Whatever it was, it was good that she's finally said something. How long has she been doing this?'

'Six months.'

'And no one knew? Not even her school?'

'Nope. No one.'

Lucas nodded. 'Well done, you, then. For picking it up and getting her to talk.'

'It wasn't exactly rocket science. And I think it was you and the cup of tea that got her to talk, wasn't it?'

He grinned. 'You think so?'

'Well, I got the impression that you were willing to sit there until two o'clock in the morning.'

'I was. Only that probably wouldn't have helped much. I was wondering whether she was going to call the police and accuse us of kidnapping.'

An involuntary shiver ran down Thea's spine. 'Don't say that.'

He gave her a querying look. 'Just a joke.'

A lot he knew. It was all too easy to get into trouble when you crossed the line between doctor and social worker. But this time it had been okay. This time Lucas had been there. She wondered if he knew just how much she appreciated that, but decided not to tell him.

CHAPTER SEVEN

Week Five

THE MONDAY MORNING meeting dealt with the practicalities, what correspondence needed to be sent out and a review of the previous week's test results. Lucas and Thea had then retreated to their desks to ponder the less straightforward matters.

'It's puzzling.' He was frowning, staring at the whiteboard on the wall, which listed all the people at the school who had tested positive.

He was in what Thea privately called 'overview mode'. She was beginning to get used to his knack of pulling back from the personal, disregarding the individual and looking at the big picture. At first she'd thought it cold—but there was an obscure symmetry in the way that Lucas's mind worked now, which she was still struggling to pin down.

'I don't know if I can help you there.'

He raised his eyebrows. 'What makes you think that?'

'Because…I'm just a working doctor. I can't see what you see in charts and paperwork.'

'The chart's meant to make it all simpler.' He studied the complex maze of blobs for individuals and different coloured lines, representing contact. 'I'll agree that it really needs to be in 3D.'

Thea chuckled. 3D wasn't going to help. 'I meant that

you seem to see trends and meanings. All I see is circles and lines.'

He shrugged. 'Helps if you let your eyes go slightly out of focus when you look at it.' He narrowed his eyes to demonstrate.

'No. It helps if you have the ability to have a kind of detachment.'

'Is that what you think?' He jerked around to face her. It was obviously still something of a sore point in Lucas's eyes. 'That I'm detached?'

'That you have the ability to step back and look at the whole problem, instead of just parts of it. I don't have that gift.'

'You have the gift of keeping me honest. You always did.' His eyes seemed to be seeing someone else. The Thea he'd first met maybe.

'You never needed to be kept honest, Lucas. You were always an idealist.' Thea wondered if she'd get the same answer that he'd given before. *I got real.*

'If you want to change the world, it helps if you know the right strings to pull.' He sighed, as if something had been lost. Shook his head slightly, as if he'd decided that it was beyond his reach. 'Returning to the matter in hand, I can't see which strings to pull here.'

Thea followed his gaze, looking at the chart again. 'Okay, so one active case, that's Derek. And eight probable latent cases, all of whom had regular contact with him.'

'And where did Derek get it from? We've confirmed that this is the same strain as the Birmingham outbreak.'

'Birmingham's not so far. People travel between there and here all the time.'

'True, but that's not the point. *Which* person in particular? I've been through all the contact information from the cases up there, and I can't find anything that links with Derek.'

'So there's someone else out there that we haven't found

yet who gave it to Derek. And he gave it to these new cases at the school.'

'Maybe. But just because the new cases are latent, it doesn't mean that they haven't had the infection for as long as Derek—just that he developed active TB and they didn't. Could be that there's another contact for one of the latent cases, who also gave it to Derek.'

'Hmm. It's a lot more difficult with these long time-scales. If you get a cold you can be pretty sure that it's the person who sneezed on you last week who gave it to you.'

He laughed. 'Maybe. Or maybe that's just our perception.'

'Don't start, Lucas, it's already complicated enough. So what do we do now?'

His eyes took on the bright gleam that was Lucas's characteristic response to a challenge. 'We try harder.'

Trying harder didn't yield any immediate results, apart from allowing them to inform two of the pupils and their families that, in the light of further tests, they were free of any infection. Which left six people, who had to be advised and reassured, and for whom an individually tailored drug regime had to be structured. It was the start of long and arduous treatment and the TB nurses would need to provide support all the way.

'You've seen Isobel?' Lucas arrived at the hospital late on Friday afternoon, after being called to a meeting elsewhere.

'Yes, I said I'd go with her to see Maggie as she didn't want to go on her own. It was a good session. Maggie's doing what she can to provide emotional and practical support for Isobel and her mother.'

'But you'll be seeing her again.' Lucas grinned at her. He already knew the answer to that.

'Yes. We have an informal arrangement. She's got my number and she'll call me and I'll take her somewhere nice for lunch. Or if she doesn't call me in the next week, I'll call her.'

'Ah. Befriending.'

'No, I like Isobel. She's got guts.'

Lucas shrugged. 'That's what befriending is, isn't it? Part of a support structure?' He was teasing her now.

'Oh, be quiet. You want an unstructured coffee break? I haven't had lunch yet.'

'Thought you'd never ask. You go on ahead, I'll just check my emails.'

Thea had only just sat down on the bench outside the cafeteria, which was rapidly becoming their place to sit. The thought unsettled her, and she wondered whether she should move. She and Lucas were just working together, and it was a temporary arrangement. They didn't have their own special places any more.

Lucas came striding towards her, frowning vigorously. He'd obviously walked straight through the cafeteria, without stopping to get himself anything to drink.

'What's up? I thought you wanted coffee?'

'There's another case.'

'What?' This was never good news, but from the look on Lucas's face it was the very worst. 'I thought we had no outstanding tests.'

'This one was picked up by her GP. He referred her on to a different hospital and the paperwork's only just come through and been connected up with our cases.'

His hand shook as he took a printed copy of an email from his pocket and handed it over. 'Her name's Safiyah Patel. Safiyah's got active pulmonary TB. It's a hard course of treatment for anyone, but at her age… She's only fourteen.'

Thea scanned the paper. 'This is Ava's school, isn't it? You know the family?'

'Yeah. I know Safiyah and her family.' There was something that Lucas was trying very hard not to say.

'Then she's a friend of Ava's.' Something cold crept into Thea's heart. Every case was personal, but this time she saw the raw edges of fear in Lucas's eyes.

A pulse beat at the side of his temple. Then suddenly he broke, all the stiff resolution seeming to drain out of him. 'I'm thinking that I should put Ava under the care of a private doctor. To avoid any conflict of interest.'

Conflict of interest didn't sound like the real reason. 'You mean that if Ava's having private treatment, she'll get better care.'

'I know what you're thinking, Thea. But Ava's my child, and I have to do the best for her that I can.'

'And what exactly am I thinking?'

He rolled his eyes. 'You're thinking about all the times we said that medicine was about need and not ability to pay. About how we said we should stick by those values.'

'I'm not thinking that at all. I'm wondering why you think that Ava's going to be better off having private treatment. Are you saying that we aren't doing the best we can for our patients?'

'No, of course not.' Anger and desperation flooded his face. 'But I don't care what's fair or what's right when it comes to Ava. I have to do what's best for her.'

'And what *is* best for her? In your considered opinion?'

He was silent for a long time. 'I can't lose her, Thea.'

'You're not going to lose her.'

'I didn't expect to lose Sam and Claire.' The haunted look in his eyes wrenched at Thea's heart.

'I think…' She paused for a moment to decide what she really did think. 'I think that's a separate thing.'

Lucas looked down at his shaking hands. 'In that case…' he took a deep breath '…take me through it. Step by step. What should I do?'

'You want me to tell you? That's one hell of a responsibility, Lucas.' This was serious. Questioning Lucas's motives was one thing. Being asked to share in a decision that involved Ava was quite another.

He nodded. 'Yeah. Tell me about it.'

'I'm not used to this.'

'Practice doesn't always make it easier.'

'All right.' She took hold of his hand, not sure whether it was to comfort him or steady her own racing heart. 'What do you think Ava would want?'

He pulled his hand away from hers. 'It doesn't matter what she wants, Thea. She's a child.'

'Yes, I know that. But I imagine she'll have an opinion, and you may as well listen to it. You don't have to do what she says.' She felt tears pricking at the sides of her eyes. This was harder than she'd imagined.

'Ava would say that it's my duty to treat her the same as everyone else. That I have to stand up and be an example to the other parents.'

'Good grief. You taught her well, then.'

He rolled his eyes. 'Yeah, I know it's my fault. Don't rub it in.'

Now he knew how she'd felt. Loving an idealist was never easy. 'All right, moving on. Do you think that our testing and treatment programme offers the best to our patients?'

'Yes. I already said that.'

'I know, just taking things in order.' She glared him into silence. 'And do you think there's anything that the private sector can offer her that we can't? Leaving the posher consulting rooms and the better coffee aside for a moment.'

He thought for a long time and then shook his head. 'Not in this case, no.'

'Right. Well, bearing all that in mind, what do you think you should do?'

He shook his head. There was another question somewhere that Thea had missed. She thought hard.

'Is it just that you feel that loving someone automatically means you have to trash your ideals?'

His lip curled suddenly. She'd hit a nerve. 'Back off, Thea.'

'Okay, okay. I'm sorry.' She felt herself flush. She hadn't meant to make this about Lucas and her. 'This is just with regard to Ava. About what's best for her.'

'Yeah. I'm sorry.' His chest heaved as he sucked in a draught of air. 'I think… Will you supervise her testing? Personally.'

'Of course. I'm going to insist on that.'

'And you'll make sure I know everything? Every last detail, even the ones that don't matter?'

'Every last one. I appreciate that you're the parent here, and I know you're worried.'

'And you'll call round this evening? If I put an extra steak on the barbecue and get a bottle of red?'

'What, in my official capacity? Not sure about that, I'll never make it round to everyone.' She grinned at him, and finally he smiled.

'As a friend. Who doesn't mind talking sense, even when I don't want to hear it?'

'I don't know. Were you thinking of getting a decent bottle of red?'

He chuckled. 'You mean not the stuff we used to drink?'

'Yes. Exactly.'

Thea grasped the heavy brass dolphin and the door swung open almost before she'd had a chance to knock on the door. Ava stepped out onto the doorstep.

'Hi. I know.'

'You know?' That statement could apply to pretty much anything.

'I know about Safiyah. I knew about it anyway because she messaged me, but her mother phoned Lucas this evening. She knows what his job is.'

'And what did Lucas say to her?' Ava didn't look overly perturbed about the situation.

'He said that Safiyah's going to be okay. That the drug regime can be tough, but that there's lots of support available, and to call if there's anything he can do.'

'Sounds good. How do you feel about that?'

'I feel sorry for Safiyah. Lucas says that as soon as she's not infectious, we'll have her and her family around for supper.'

'Well, I'm sure that'll cheer her up a bit.'

Ava rolled her eyes. 'All the other parents will be looking to see what he does. I told him that, and that I was pleased he was setting a good example.'

Thea suppressed a smile. 'Good for you.'

'Then he gave me *the talk.*' Ava sighed. She and Lucas clearly had regular *talks.* 'He asked me how I was feeling and I told him I was feeling fine. So he said that I wasn't to worry, and that Safiyah was going to be all right, and that TB isn't easily transmitted from one person to another.'

'And what did you say?' Thea couldn't contain her smile.

'I said I already knew that. There's plenty of information on the internet and I can read.'

'And...what did he say?'

'He just nodded, and went into the kitchen and poured himself a glass of wine. I'd get in there quickly if you want any, before he drinks the lot.'

'Okay, thanks. Is that all?'

Ava nodded. 'Yes. Come in.'

Lucas was at the barbecue, nursing a half-empty glass of red wine and looking remarkably cheerful after the rigours of *the talk.* Leaving the steak to sizzle for a few moments, he strode inside and poured a generous measure for Thea.

'Careful, I'm driving.' Without thinking, she topped his glass up from her own. Those little acts of intimacy that had survived the years and needed to be unlearnt.

'She knows.' He leaned towards her confidingly.

'Yes, I know she knows. Now that everybody knows, can we all stop whispering about it, please? And why are you smirking?'

'I wouldn't call it smirking. I'm just reflecting on the fact that Ava's information dissemination techniques are second only to your own.'

'What's that supposed to mean?'

'It's a compliment. And, by the way, thank you. I nearly made a fool of myself there.'

'It wasn't foolish to be concerned about Ava.'

Lucas cut her short with a shake of his head. 'It's not a matter of concern. The best thing I can teach Ava is that I know how to stand by my principles. And I do honestly believe that we do the best we can for the kids in our care and that she'll get no better treatment elsewhere.'

Lucas gave his most seductive smile, and Thea felt her knees begin to shake.

'Do I smell burning?' She nodded towards the barbecue and he darted back outside, flipping the steaks over adroitly. Ava appeared, making a beeline for him.

'Thea agrees with me. You're doing the right thing.'

Lucas feigned incomprehension and then gave in. 'Thanks. Nice to know.'

And the matter was closed. Until after dinner, when Lucas leaned back in his chair on the patio, ruminating on the problem.

'So we have two separate nodes of infection.'

'Only they probably aren't separate at all. We just can't see the link.' Thea had been thinking about that too.

'Yeah. And whoever the link is, they're going untreated.' One of his fingers tapped restlessly on the arm of his chair. Lucas wasn't going to let this go until he'd found that person.

'So what do we know?'

'We have two schools, six miles apart. Very different

communities, and it's not that likely that the kids from one school mix much with the kids from the other.'

'Maybe inter-school activities?'

'Perhaps. But would that provide the degree of exposure needed to infect someone?'

'Does she have a boyfriend?'

'Don't think so, her parents are pretty strict about that kind of thing...' He paused to think. 'I wouldn't be the one to know that, would I?'

'Not necessarily.'

Lucas frowned. 'It's the end of term in six weeks as well. That's going to make things more difficult, at the moment everyone's pretty much in the same place. Once school breaks up people will be going away on holiday and it'll be more difficult to contact them.'

'So we've got our golden opportunity now. Let's make the most of it.'

'Yeah. Let's do that.' He stared out over the garden. 'By the way, are you free this weekend?'

'I was going to work anyway—there's something you want me to do?'

'Actually, I was going to try and stop you from working. You look tired and we all need a break.'

Looking tired probably wasn't the best of impressions to make, but it was nice that he'd noticed. 'What kind of break?'

'I've got to go shopping with Ava. They have an end-of-term dance, and this year she wants a nice dress. I wondered if you'd like to come. I dare say that your opinion would count for a little more than mine.'

'Ava wants me to go?'

His gaze met hers, and the old electricity suddenly zipped between them. '*I* want you to come. I'm shamelessly using Ava as an excuse.'

It was impossible to refuse. Maybe this was the start of what she'd hoped would happen someday. Maybe she was moving on from the past and maybe, just maybe, Lucas could be a part of her future.

'All right. What time?'

'About ten-ish?'

'Ten's good. I'll come over and meet you here.'

CHAPTER EIGHT

LUCAS HAD UNDERESTIMATED himself. He was every girl's dream as a shopping companion. Ava had been given a generous budget, and instead of loitering around, waiting for her to make her choice, Lucas was in the thick of it all, making suggestions and looking through rails of dresses.

Thea, on the other hand, didn't feel as if she was a great deal of help. When she pulled a dark blue, long-sleeved dress from the rail, both Lucas and Ava wrinkled their noses at the same time.

Finally, six dresses were selected and Ava was despatched to the changing room.

'You used to love clothes shopping.' He looked speculatively at Thea.

'You used to hate it.'

He chuckled. 'I learned. What did you do?'

'Unlearned?'

Ava's appearance in a red and white patterned summer dress diverted his attention. 'Turn around.' He considered for a moment. 'It's a nice dress, but it's not really an evening dress. And it doesn't do that much for you.'

What he meant was that the sleeveless dress, cut to flatter the curves of a slightly rounder figure than Ava's, was a bit too old for her. Thea mentally congratulated him on his tact.

'That's what I thought. It would be good to get a nice

summer dress for the holidays, though.' Ava shot him a wheedling look.

'Yes, you do need one. We'll have a look, see what they have.' Lucas waved her back into the changing room. 'Try the next one.'

'That's downright unnatural.' Ava had disappeared back into the changing room and Thea leaned towards Lucas.

'What? You didn't think it was too old for her?' Lucas's eyes had a hint of mischief in them.

'Yes, much too old. What's unnatural is you sitting here, making helpful suggestions, instead of hanging around in a corner somewhere, wishing that this was all over so we could go and get lunch in the pub.'

'Things change. And lunch in the pub doesn't sound too bad either.' His assessing gaze swept over Thea, so intense that it was almost a physical touch. 'Actually, the dress would suit you.'

'I don't wear dresses much these days.' Never, actually.

His eye surveyed her jeans and grey hooded top. 'Shame.'

Before she could tell him it was just a matter of practicality, he was on his feet, scanning the rails of dresses. Ava appeared again from the dressing room, looking surly in the extreme, in a white ruffled concoction.

'No. Definitely not. It makes you look like a Christmas cake.' Thea gave her opinion and Ava giggled.

'Where's Lucas?'

'Gone to find you another dress.'

Ava grinned. 'Will you help me with the next one?'

'Yes, of course.'

The next dress was a plain, wrap-around style, which gaped a little at the front. 'This is no good. My bra's showing.' Ava pulled the dress this way and that miserably.

'It just needs a pin. Look.' Thea held the neckline of the dress so that it wrapped interestingly, rather than plunging dangerously.

Ava thought about it, and then nodded. 'I really like that.'

A couple of other women, obviously in the changing room for consultation rather than to buy, expressed their approval and someone produced a safety pin. Lucas was shown the dress and told Ava she looked gorgeous, and once that was settled Ava tried on a couple of other summer dresses, settling on a pinky-purple shift dress that suited her dark hair and eyes.

'Now you.' It seemed that Lucas wasn't going to let Thea off the hook and he handed her the red dress. Distressingly, he seemed to have estimated her size correctly.

'I don't think so.'

'Go on. It'll look great on you.' His eyes dared her to do it. 'Just try it. What's the harm?'

Plenty that couldn't be voiced and nothing that could. And Lucas made her feel safe. He couldn't help it and neither could she, it was just one of those things. Thea turned and walked into the dressing room.

She almost chickened out. In the mirror, her legs looked too pale, her arms too thin, and having habitually worn trousers for so long, a dress seemed unbearably revealing. But this was Lucas she was up against.

'Fabulous. You look gorgeous, doesn't she, Ava?'

'Yep. Wish I had curves.'

'Give it time.' Lucas grinned at her.

'It doesn't feel quite right.' Thea tugged self-consciously at the skirt, her bare toes curling with embarrassment.

'That's because you need red shoes to go with it. For dancing.'

Her heart suddenly melted. Not exactly taking all her fears with it but overwriting them with remembered joy. The red shoes that Lucas had always referred to as her dancing shoes had been her favourites. She'd danced in them, thrown them off to follow him across moonlit grass, and on more than one occasion had made love in them.

'You think so?'

'Don't you go dancing any more?'

As it happened, no. Thea hesitated.

'Buy the dress.' He gave her an imploring look, as if his whole world would fall apart if she didn't.

'Buy it for her. Where are your manners?' Ava's voice broke in and both of them ignored her. Lucas would have bought her the dress in a heartbeat, but he wanted her to want it. When he looked at her like that, she almost did.

'I'll—'

'Buy it.'

'Okay. I'll buy it.'

She didn't have time to go back into the changing room and think of a reason to change her mind. Lucas picked her up and carried her to the cash desk, subjecting the cashier to the killer smile that generally let him get away with almost anything.

'Would you mind scanning the lady, please?' He leaned over so that the woman could reach the ticket, which was hanging from Thea's shoulder.

'*Sorry.*' Thea mouthed the word, feeling herself blush, and hung on tight to Lucas.

'Would you like a bag?' The woman was grinning.

'Yes, please. And…' Lucas looked around for Ava and found her standing behind him, clutching her own purchases. 'These two as well, please.'

'You can put me down now,' Thea whispered in his ear, and he ignored her. Ava pulled his wallet from his back pocket and handed over his card, and in a show of bravado he kept hold of Thea at the same time as punching his pin number into the machine.

'Enjoy.' The cashier handed Ava's bag over and grinned at Thea. 'Would you like me to take the tag off?'

'No, thanks. I'm going to get changed now.' Thea pushed at Lucas's shoulders. He could let her down now.

'Not until we've got the right shoes.' Lucas was obviously on a mission.

'Second floor.'

'Thank you.' Lucas allowed Thea to slip down out of his arms. 'Let's go.'

When she collected her jeans and top from the changing room, they seemed suddenly drab and unexciting. Thea took a moment to smooth the red dress over her hips. It was lovely.

Lucas hustled her barefoot to the second floor then applied himself to talking Ava out of a succession of unsuitable shoes. Thea was left to scan the shelves on her own.

Red shoes. She reached towards the pair of red strappy sandals, almost afraid to touch them. She had to have something now that Lucas had bought the dress. And these were so very pretty.

She sat down next to Lucas and asked for the shoes in her size. 'You like these?'

'Do you?'

'Yes, I like them.' She stood and took a turn around the seating area. 'They're very comfortable.'

'I like them too.' He nodded in approval and reached for his wallet, but this time Thea was too quick for him. Pulling the shoes off, she made the cash desk in her bare feet.

'Pipped to the post.' She could feel him behind her. Not quite touching her but somehow managing to make her feel as if he was.

'Yeah. It's all for the best.' She turned in the confined space between the counter and his body, and faced him. Lucas didn't back off. 'If you bought them for me then you wouldn't know if I was just being nice by wearing them.'

'True. Are you thinking of being nice to me, then?'

Who couldn't when Lucas was in this mood? Playful, unpredictable and devastatingly attractive. 'Maybe. Maybe not.'

It was an unashamed come-on and a smile tugged at his mouth in response. 'I'll be waiting to see...'

It was just a simple, sleeveless summer dress, red flowers on a white background, but Thea looked lovely in it. The curve of her shoulder. Her knees. Lucas hadn't thought he had a thing about knees.

He had thought he'd left all this behind, but that had been before he'd seen Thea in the dress. It wasn't so much the dress but the certain knowledge that she hadn't changed at all really. Along with the answering realisation that he hadn't changed as much as he'd thought either. Maybe he could leave the past behind and be the man she deserved. Right now, he reckoned that was a possibility.

'Isn't Ava coming with us?' She'd accepted his offer of dinner, and seemed surprised when she heard the front door slam.

'No, she's going next door, to my parents'. She plays bridge with my dad on a Saturday evening sometimes.'

She raised one eyebrow. 'She plays bridge. With your father?'

'Yeah, she's really good at it. I don't know what she sees in it personally, but...' Lucas shrugged. 'Are you ready?'

'Yes. Where are we going?' She picked up the cardigan that Ava had lent her in case the evening became too chilly for just a summer dress and red shoes. Lucas could have thought of a better way to keep her warm, but he had to admit that Ava's approach was more practical.

'I've nothing in mind. Shall we go with the flow?' For the last seven years he'd known exactly where he was going, what route he would take and what time he was expected back. Even if they were just going out for a bite to eat, going with the flow seemed deliciously like old times.

'Sounds good.'

* * *

They'd decided on a Greek restaurant, a little off the beaten track. Sitting at a small wobbly table, they feasted on fresh sardines, baked with oregano and lemon juice and served with salad.

'First impressions.' She grinned at him and Lucas remembered the old game they used to play. 'Greece.'

'The sky. And the turquoise blue sea.'

She nodded. 'France?'

'That blasted ferry. When we got stuck for hours.' She laughed at the memory and Lucas tried one of his own. 'Bangladesh?'

She thought for a moment. 'Colour. Wonderful henna shades that you don't find here. Heat. Gastroenteritis.'

'You were sick?'

'Not the first time.' Lucas could see by the flash of alarm in her eyes that she'd already said more than she meant to.

'You've been more than once?'

'Yes.'

'You never mentioned it.'

She raised an eyebrow in surprise. Had she thought for one minute that he hadn't been paying attention these past weeks? 'Didn't I?'

Her attention was diverted by a clatter in the corner, or maybe she just wanted to change the subject. 'Looks as if there's going to be singing.' A young man was fussing over the setting up of a microphone and the positioning of speakers.

When the bouzouki began to play, there was little prospect of any more conversation. Lucas pulled his chair around next to hers to watch the dancing, and the waiter delivered two small cups of wickedly strong espresso with tall glasses of water.

She looked so beautiful, and the beat of the music was insistent. Lucas could do nothing else. He got to his feet, taking Thea's hand, and asked her to dance. Then she was in his arms in the cramped space, bumping into tables and avoiding the feet of other dancers. Bliss. Pure, unadulterated bliss.

Thea blamed it on the red shoes. Or the music, or the sudden release from day-to-day cares that sometimes seemed to be all there was to life. At the moment, she wasn't ready to shoulder any of the blame herself.

Just for tonight no one could refuse to dance when they were wearing red shoes, and no one could sit down again after the first dance, even if it did last for a good ten minutes, the singers clearly reluctant to allow the crush of dancers to rest. It might be more like an assault course than a dance floor, but Lucas was there. The rhythm of his body still remembered after all these years. His smell. The way he pulled her in, his hand resting lightly on her waist but somehow managing to insinuate that it might move at any moment and then she'd be lost.

Finally the singer took a break and made for the bar. As an impromptu karaoke session got started, Lucas paid the bill and walked her to the car, opening the passenger door and helping her in, even though she could manage perfectly well for herself.

He switched the radio on, and music came from four directions. Late-night songs in the car. They'd used to wind the windows down and bawl the words out together. Now it was a little different.

Suddenly the car screeched to a halt. The opening bars of a familiar song were playing and Lucas turned the volume up. Then he was at the passenger door and beckoning her out of her seat.

'Lucas, no.' People passing by on the wide pavement were already looking their way.

'Tell me again. You could try making it a little more convincing this time.'

She couldn't. Not tonight. When she got out of the car

she found herself in his arms. And now that she wasn't concentrating on not bumping into anyone else, there was only Lucas.

Her hand moved to his shoulder, her fingers delighting in the smooth ripple of movement. He'd filled out since they'd danced all night together, but all of it was muscle. And he hadn't lost any of the supple rhythm, which had delighted her so then and which made it impossible for her to refuse him now.

'People are looking.' She rested her head against his chest.

'What people?'

'I don't know.' They were somewhere else, on an uneventful Saturday evening, staring as two people danced together on the street. As far away from them as if they were in another dimension.

'Since we're alone...can you still dip?'

'I can dip. Further than you can, any day. You're not as young as you were.'

She felt a chuckle reverberate through his chest. 'I don't think so.'

'You're just too afraid to find out.'

That was the way it had always been with her and Lucas. He would dare something, and she'd dare him back, an inch further. It could be pleasure or work, but the same rules always applied. He'd take her to the very edge, but he'd be there with her, protecting her.

'Ready?' His lips brushed her ear and she shivered.

'Are you?'

She knew just when the beat of the song would allow for a long, low dip. He bent her backwards, holding her tight. As she felt her balance change, one leg curled around his, and her body moved tight against his. It was no surprise to find that he was just as aroused as she was.

'That all you can manage?'

In answer, he tipped her back another couple of inches,

and she felt his lips brush against her neck. Then she was back straight again, pressed helplessly against him, caught in Lucas and the music.

'Good to see you're still up for making a spectacle of yourself,' he whispered into her ear, and suddenly the world jolted back into sharp focus. Passers-by were slowing to look, and one couple had even stopped briefly and added a couple of dance steps of their own to the mix. People were smiling.

She nestled in close to Lucas, safe in his arms. Somehow the looks of these strangers weren't so bad with him there to protect her. The song on the radio segued into another old favourite and she stayed right where she was.

'You want to come back to mine?'

'I have to. My other clothes are still in Ava's room.' Folded neatly on a chair, beckoning her back into reality.

'That's not an answer. Do you *want* to come back? Ava's staying over with my parents, she always does after bridge nights.'

'For coffee?'

'Yeah, for coffee.' He leaned in close again. 'My coffee's not only fair trade, it's also made completely without expectations.'

The choice of whether this evening would finish in his bed or whether they'd remain old acquaintances, catching up on lost time, was clearly hers. And perhaps they were old enough friends to be able to do that and not face the consequences.

'Okay, then. Let's find out what expectation-free coffee tastes like.'

He chuckled quietly, circling back towards the open door of the car. 'Yeah. Let's find out.'

CHAPTER NINE

THEY SAT ON the patio, separated by two glasses of champagne and a large bowl of strawberries. Thea pulled the stalk from one, and dropped it into her glass, and Lucas winced.

'You always did know how to ruin a good glass of champagne.'

She laughed. 'I like way it makes the bubbles smell. And the contents of your fridge have definitely improved over the years.'

'More spare cash. And having a teenager in the house. When Ava's friends come over, it's like being invaded by locusts.'

'And they have strawberries and champagne?' Thea was teasing, but she wanted to know who else Lucas might have had in mind when he'd bought the bottle that he'd drawn out from under the kitchen counter and put to chill.

He chuckled and provided the answer she was looking for. 'The champagne's left over from the party we threw when my dad retired, two years ago.'

'He retired? He always seemed so involved with his law practice.'

'It was his baby. He founded it and built it up, and he loved the law. But when Sam died and Mum got sick, he changed. When sixty came round, he said that he wanted to concentrate on the family.'

'I can understand that. The decision worked for him?'

'Yeah. It worked for him.'

They sat for a while in companionable silence. Thea slipped off her shoes, brushing her toes across the rough paving stones, shivering as the cool kiss of the evening air touched her arms.

'Cold? I'll fetch you a sweater.'

It was now or never, and suddenly *never again* seemed too hard to contemplate. Her gaze found his, and they were locked together, each understanding what the other wanted.

'Or you could come here. I'll keep you warm.' His lips curved into a smile, and when Thea rounded the table to stand between his outstretched legs, he reached for her, pulling her down onto his lap.

'That's better.' She curled up in his arms.

'Much.' He reached for her champagne. 'Drink?'

'Yes.' Thea grinned and tapped her mouth with one finger. 'Right there.'

'Your wish…' He left the sentence unfinished but there was no doubt that whatever she wanted *was* his command right now. He held the glass to her lips, and she took a sip.

'Thank you. Strawberry?'

'Thought you'd never ask.'

She leaned forward, finding the best in the bowl and hulling it carefully, letting him watch and wait. He took a bite and she caught the juice that dribbled down his chin with her finger. She brushed the remainder of the fruit against his lips, snatching it away when he opened his mouth, and popping it into her own.

'Oh! So that's the way it goes, eh?' He caught her wrist, pulling her hand back to his mouth and sucking the last remains of the juice from her fingers. 'You taste sweet.'

Slowly he reached for her, each second a jewel, sparkling in the darkness. He kissed her, a delicious cocktail of tenderness and longing. Lucas knew her better than any man alive, and he could touch her soul if he wanted to. That kiss made it very clear that he did want to.

She was almost afraid.

Forget the *almost*. She was afraid. Losing Lucas the first time had broken her heart. Taking him back only put her in the firing line all over again.

She tasted of strawberries and champagne, and something warm and wild, which stripped away everything other than the urgent need to lie down beside her. He felt her tremble in his arms, and he told himself that was just the emotion of the moment. Then she hesitated.

He knew her too well. When Thea made up her mind to do something, she didn't hesitate, not unless she was playing for time. She kissed him again, but drew back almost immediately.

'What's the matter?'

She seemed almost not to hear him for a moment. Never a good sign.

'Nothing.'

He curled his arms around her, holding her tight against his chest. It was time for a bit of honesty. 'You think this is a mistake, don't you?'

'Not necessarily.' She didn't move. 'I've made worse.'

'That's good to know. What do you class as a worse mistake than sleeping with me?'

She laughed quietly. 'There are lots of mistakes worse than that.'

'Yeah, right.' Something was wrong. Something that she wouldn't talk about. 'Tell me, Thea.'

'Tell you what?' She tried to pretend that she didn't know what he was talking about.

'You know. Tell me.'

She was on her feet now, stepping over the stone kerb of the patio and onto the grass. Thea always had liked walk-

ing barefoot on grass. She took a couple of paces and then
turned back towards him. 'Nothing. There's nothing.'

'I don't believe you.'

Something about the way she was meandering back and
forth on the grass in front of him, like a broken doll, drove
Lucas to his feet. He tried to catch her hand but she spun
away from him, stretching her arms out, as if she were a
wraith that could melt into the cool night air.

'I'm an ex-con. You know that?' There was a sad, mock-
ing tone to her voice. Something that spoke of unbearable
misery.

He could back off and hope she snapped out of this...
No. He'd backed away once, when her friends had told him
she didn't want to speak to him. That was a mistake that
Lucas never could—never would—repeat.

'Thea. Stop it.' He took her firmly by the shoulders.
'Stop it now. Nothing's so bad that you have to walk away
from me. There's nothing you can tell me that I won't understand.'

'Maybe *I* don't understand.' She was shivering now in
the chill of the night, but her eyes were focussed on his
face. The Thea who had retreated from him was battling
her way back to the surface.

'Then perhaps I can. Give me a chance, and I won't let
you down.' He wrapped his arms around her.

'I'm cold, Lucas.'

'Come inside, then.'

She followed him through the kitchen and into the sitting
room, curling her legs underneath her as she sat down in
a chair by the fireplace. She seemed to be holding herself
together, and Lucas hoped that she wouldn't draw back at
the last moment.

'When I went to Bangladesh, I knew I had to go back.
It's a place of so many opposites. The people there...there's
so much that they need, and yet in some ways they have
more than we do.'

'And you did. Go back?'

She nodded, staring at her hands in her lap. 'Yes, I did my two year foundation training in Leicester, and I went back. I worked in a TB clinic in a rural area near Dhaka for two years. It was harder than I could ever have imagined, and more rewarding than I could have ever dreamed.'

'If I say that I envied you…'

She looked up at him. 'Then I'd say that you haven't heard the whole story. One evening a young girl came to the clinic. She'd run away from her husband, who'd beaten her pretty badly. She'd run away before, back to her family, but they'd sent her back to him. She was fifteen years old, and pregnant.'

'What did you do?' Lucas tried to drive the image of Ava from his head. Just a year younger than a girl who'd seen more than anyone should have to.

'I should have passed her over to the hospital authorities and let them work things out.' She shrugged. 'As foreign aid workers, we had to be careful not to interfere in cultural matters. But I knew that she'd probably end up either back with her husband or in disgrace with her family, and I couldn't just watch that happen. So I hid her.'

'Where?'

'I was living in a house with two Australian nurses. They were both away so I took her home. Gave her something to eat and put her to bed. She was so frightened that I'd turn her over to the police; her husband's cousin was the chief of police for the area. I found a women's shelter in Dhaka and arranged a place for her there, and two days later I borrowed a car and took her to the railway station. I bought her a ticket and gave her what money I had, and put her on the train.'

'So she got away safely?' Lucas was clawing for some part of a happy ending here, because he knew from Thea's face that there was more, and it wasn't good.

'I don't know. The woman from the shelter was meant to

be meeting her at the other end…' She shrugged. 'I never knew. Her husband had come to the clinic, looking for her, and I thought I'd done a pretty good job of convincing him that I didn't know where she was. But when I arrived back from the station he'd called in the police and they'd searched the house. They arrested me.'

'For helping a fifteen-year-old girl who shouldn't have been married in the first place?'

'It happens. The official marriage age in Bangladesh for girls is eighteen, but fifty per cent of young women are married before that age.' Her voice became calm. As if the cold, hard statistic was somehow protecting her.

She couldn't retreat from it now. Somehow he had to keep her in touch with her feelings, however devastating.

'What happened to you then?' She shook her head, and Lucas rose, kneeling in front of her, taking hold of her hand. 'What happened to you then, Thea?'

'They locked me up. The husband said I'd kidnapped the girl.'

'What was her name, Thea? Say her name.'

The pain in her eyes was almost unbearable. 'Ayesha.'

'And they wanted you to tell them where she was?'

'Yes. They questioned me the next day, for hours. They said I'd be charged and I'd go to prison for a long time.'

'Did they hurt you?'

She looked up at him, a ghost of a grim smile on her face. 'No, they didn't beat me up or anything. Prisons and police cells in Bangladesh aren't very nice places, but they treated me fairly and I had a lawyer. Not that he did very much. Just told me that I ought to say where Ayesha was.'

Perhaps this was the thing that she'd hidden all these years. The guilt of betraying a helpless child.

'I'm not sure I would have been brave enough to even try to hold out against them.'

'I knew that if it ever came to trial I'd have to defend myself. But in the meantime I tried to convince myself that

I really didn't know where she was. Repeated it to myself over and over again at night.'

The words hit Lucas like a blow to the chest. Thea hadn't told them. She'd locked herself away behind a protective shell, which had become as much of a prison to her as physical walls. 'How long…?'

'Two weeks. It wasn't so bad.'

'Don't say that. I'm not stupid, I know it must have been horrible.'

She nodded. 'There were rats. At night they used to turn the lights out and I could hear them scratching in the dark. I just had a mattress to sleep on, and it smelled. There wasn't enough water to wash properly. And they just kept shouting questions at me.'

She covered her ears, squeezing her eyes shut, as if to block it all out. Lucas pulled her towards him, holding her tight. 'It's all right. It's okay, Thea. You're safe now.'

'No. I'll never be safe. You don't understand.'

Holding her now was too little and too late, but it was all he could do. 'You did a very brave thing, Thea. I couldn't have done it.'

'Yes, you could.' Her voice was quiet, expressionless again. 'It's what you would have done. I told myself that.'

Lucas choked. She'd turned him into some kind of hero, someone to follow and look up to. And in reality he was the worst kind of villain. 'Dear God, Thea…'

She pulled away from him so that she could see his face. 'Isn't it what you would have done?'

Lucas let go of his pride. Without as much as a wave goodbye. 'I don't know. It's easy to say what's right and wrong now, but in that situation, under that kind of pressure, no one knows what they'd do. All I know is that you did what I would have wanted myself to do. Something that I'd have been proud to have done.'

She stiffened suddenly, pushing him away. 'No, you wouldn't. You don't understand.'

It all seemed shockingly clear in his head. He'd driven her away, and she'd paid the price for it. He should tell her that. Find some way to apologise, even if words were never going to be enough.

Lucas hesitated, and in that moment everything was lost. She slipped away from him, almost running for the front door, tearing at the lock and wrenching it open. Her car was only a few steps across the gravel. She got in, yanking the door closed, and started the engine.

All Thea wanted to do was to get away from him. If she was alone, she could get everything back under control again. Stop the feelings that threatened to engulf her.

She switched the headlights on and saw him, blinded by the light, standing right in her path. She'd backed the car into the shade of a tree when she'd arrived that morning, and her only way out was forward.

'Get out of the way, Lucas.' She muttered the words, smacking her hand on the horn. When he didn't move, desperation began to claw at her and she wound the window down. 'I'll run you down if you don't move.'

'Go on, then.'

Perhaps he thought she wouldn't. She let go of the handbrake and the car slid forward a couple of inches before she slammed her foot on the brake. Perhaps he was right.

He fell to his knees. Not the smartest of things to do, in the path of a car driven by someone frantic with remembered grief and anger and who had nowhere else to run. She pulled the handbrake up as tight as it would go and switched the engine off.

He didn't move so she got out of the car, the gravel from the drive digging painfully into her bare feet. Walked over to him with as much dignity as she could manage. 'Lucas, this is crazy.'

'No. It's not. I know there's more. You have to tell someone. And I need to know.'

'Why?'

He didn't answer for a moment and she turned away from him. Suddenly he was on his feet.

'Because it was my fault. I lied to you. I always meant to go to Bangladesh on my own. When you told me that I thought that I had to trash my ideals in order to love someone, you were right. I chose my ideals over you. I never thought you'd put your own career on hold and come with me.'

She'd always wondered. Now that Lucas had said it, it almost came as a relief. 'You thought wrong, then.'

'Yes, I did. It's not your fault that you ended up in that cell. It's mine.'

'You're overestimating yourself, Lucas. You can't assume that you're responsible for everything I did since you left. I do have some hand in my own life.' Hadn't she been thinking the same as him all along? That if Lucas had been there it would have been different? She wouldn't have got herself into that mess, or, if she had, he would have been there and helped her out of it.

He didn't seem to be listening. 'I won't let you go this time, Thea. We're going to go inside and you'll tell the rest of it. I know there's more.'

'It's of no consequence. Let it go.'

She didn't really want him to let it go. Didn't want him to let *her* go. When he took her hand, she let him lead her into the house. He shut the door on the darkness outside and walked behind her into the sitting room. Then he waited.

It was as if someone else was speaking. Someone who loved and trusted the man sitting beside her. 'The other workers at the clinic got me a lawyer from Dhaka, a really good man. He found someone to back up my story that Ayesha had run away, and he got me out. Then it started.' Thea felt herself start to tremble uncontrollably.

'Okay, sweetheart. Take a breath. Take it slowly.'

He held her hand, counting out the breaths for her. Finally her heart began to stop thumping in her chest.

'Everyone knew what had happened. The local press were waiting outside the police station, and when I wouldn't answer any questions they shouted at me. They called me...' The words stuck in her throat and she started to panic again.

'Okay. I've got the picture. What happened then?'

'It got worse. When I wouldn't talk to the press, they spoke to the director of the clinic, and he said that what I'd done was culturally insensitive. They went to town with that and started printing all kinds of lies. That I'd sent her to the city to fend for herself, that I was involved in a prostitution racket even. There were groups of men outside the house, shouting and throwing things. Someone poured...' She choked on the remembered smell. 'You don't want to know what they poured through the kitchen window.'

He was shaking his head in disbelief. 'And they drove you out.'

'I wanted to stay and explain, but the director came to the house after about a week. Gave me two hours to pack, and then drove me to Dhaka and put me on a plane.' She shrugged miserably. 'Maybe there was nothing to explain. I have no idea what happened to Ayesha. Maybe I just made things worse for her, I'll never know.'

'You tried, Thea. You saw a young girl, suffering terribly and you helped her. If the people who bullied you won't let you be proud of yourself for that, then let me be proud for you. Because I am. More than I can say.'

The sincerity in his voice seemed to drown out all those other voices. She wound her arms around his shoulders, yanking him roughly towards her. She heard his sharp, exhaled breath and then felt him holding her, gently at first and then hard and tight. She knew from the tremble of his body that he was weeping silently.

This was her safe place. It was the one she'd been looking for all this time. It was the place that she could finally cry. When there was no more strength left for tears they just held each other.

'Did you know that I'm going back?' Just saying it made it seem a little less challenging.

'Back? Where?'

'To Asia. You know that Michael put a condition on my leading the TB team?'

He nodded. 'I heard something about it. You're writing a paper on the work.'

'I'm presenting it. At a conference. It's in India.'

'The one in September?'

She'd been trying not to think about it, but suddenly it all seemed real. 'Maybe I'll think of a way to get out of it. Break my leg and miss my plane?' She grinned, but it didn't seem like much of a joke.

Lucas wasn't smiling. 'Maybe you need to go.'

'Maybe I do. I don't want to, though.'

'I'm booked to go to that conference. I don't have my flights yet so maybe we could travel out there together.'

A faint echo of the last time that she'd hoped to meet Lucas at the airport made her shiver.

But if she couldn't find an excuse to get out of going, then this actually didn't seem like too bad an option. At least there would be someone she knew there. 'Okay. *If* I go.'

Lucas narrowed his eyes, as if he was about to press the point, but seemed to realise that Thea didn't want to talk any more. 'Think about it. Where are your jeans?'

'I left them in Ava's room when I changed to go out. Why?'

'Go and put them on.'

CHAPTER TEN

LUCAS, AS USUAL, had managed to get things exactly right. A gesture that was somewhere between spending the night together and letting her go home. He caught her hand and led her across the lawn, which stretched across from the back of both his house and his parents' house next door.

'Where are we going?' she whispered into the darkness. Not that she really cared, she would have gone anywhere with him at this moment.

'Remember the tree house?'

'The one that your dad built for you and Sam? That you nearly fell out of that time…' They'd sneaked outside, at two in the morning, climbed the tree and Lucas had laid a blanket down on the wooden platform. Hidden from view, they'd curled up together, listening to the sounds of the night and the rustle of the leaves over their heads.

'I didn't fall; I was trying to get out of the way of your elbows. Anyway, it's undergone something of an upgrade since then.'

He stopped at the foot of the oak tree, next to a pile of large floor cushions and a box, which he must have carried out there while she'd been upstairs. Lucas tested his weight on the sturdy framework that ran up the side of the trunk, and disappeared up into the branches.

'Pass me the box.' His hand appeared, reaching down, and Thea held the box up over her head, feeling him lift it out of her hands. A moment of stillness, there in the dark, and then light glimmered from the branches.

'Now the rest.'

The cushions were large and unwieldy, but she held them up, feeling him take their weight. Then the bundle that lay beneath them, a throw, wrapped together with a roll-up mattress and a waterproof sheet. Another pause, and then Lucas reappeared, climbing back down.

'Now you. Can you climb?'

Of course she could, but she let him guide her up the framework of steps just for the sheer pleasure of it. As they got up amongst the branches she could see the platform, still there and now surrounded by sturdy guardrails.

'Ava uses this in the summer. She and her friends go up there and… I don't know what they do. Play bridge, probably.'

'No boys?'

'No boys. This is a women-only tree. Apart from me, that is.'

'One rule for her and another for you?'

'Yep. That's the way it goes.' Lucas guided her forward and she climbed over the guardrail, her feet meeting softness. Lucas had spread the mattress over the wooden platform and it was strewn with cushions. Shot silk and gold thread gave a rich, sumptuous feel to the fabrics, and above her head a light glimmered.

'What is that doing there?'

'Seemed like the right place for it.'

Not many trees could boast a chandelier suspended in their branches, let alone one that lit up. 'Suppose so.'

'We found it in a junk shop. It polished up quite well, don't you think?'

'It's lovely. I like the red sparklies.' Thea craned up to see where the cable that ran from the top went.

'There's a solar panel further up. You just have to hang the chandelier and clip the cable on.' Lucas guided her over the rails and onto the platform. 'Make yourself comfortable.'

Thea sat down. The night was still warm, and the twisted branches over her head seemed to curl protectively around her. Nothing could touch her here. The leaves rustled as the breeze caught them and the red glass hanging from the chandelier tinkled. She slipped off her shoes, and stretched out on the cushions.

He levered himself up, and onto the platform next to her. 'You like it?'

'I love it. It's so peaceful up here. It feels like a secret place, where the world can't find us.'

In the half-light his face seemed even more handsome. The worry lines that creased his brow had softened, and his smile seemed warmer somehow. Lucas reached for her, and she curled into his arms.

Lucas was dimly aware of the breeze on his face and the sun, somewhere beyond his closed eyelids. And that there was a warm body next to him. He moved on the makeshift nest of cushions, and Thea stirred then settled back into sleep.

He'd thought about this often. He hadn't reckoned on it ever happening again, and certainly not quite like this, but the warm remembrance of waking up with her had never quite left him. He'd missed the sex but he'd reconciled himself to that loss. Now he realised that the thing he'd really never come to terms with losing was waking up with Thea.

His shoulder ached, and he'd lost the feeling in one arm. Gingerly he slid it out from under her, and she shifted again. Then her eyes opened.

He'd wondered if she might not remember where she was and start to panic. But she just smiled sleepily. 'Hello.'

'Hey. All right?'

'Mmm. It's nice and warm up here.' She snuggled against him under the quilt. 'Are you warm enough?'

'Yes.' Lucas curled his legs up to slide his feet under the covers and felt them tangle with hers. Felt her toes brush against his.

'Ow. Your feet are freezing!' He felt her foot rub against his. 'I'll warm them up.'

He found himself laughing quietly, at the pure joy of it all. He hadn't quite meant for them to finish up like this but, then, he hadn't meant for them not to either. All he'd known last night had been that she shouldn't be alone, that she'd needed a friend and not a lover. And this old tree had been a place of refuge for him all his life.

'What's the time?' Her fingers curled around his wrist, and he moved his arm so she could see his wristwatch. Such a little thing, but one of the many little things he remembered her doing when they'd been together. Lucas's heart almost exploded out of his chest.

'It's early. Seven o'clock.' She put his arm back where she'd found it.

'We're okay for another couple of hours, then. Ava never surfaces before ten on a Sunday and Mum and Dad like a lie-in too.'

'So they won't catch us here.'

'No. No one'll catch us. Go back to sleep. I'll go and get some coffee.'

She laughed sleepily. 'Bet you spill it, climbing back up again.'

'You want coffee up here?' Lucas had intended to set the table in the kitchen and cook breakfast for her.

'Of course I do.'

'Then I'll just have to be careful, won't I?' Lucas untangled himself from her limbs, tucking the quilt around her, and found his shoes. While the coffee was brewing, he'd find the booking form for that conference in India and put it in his briefcase. He'd need to get that off on Monday morning if he was to be sure of a place.

* * *

Fresh coffee and warm croissants, in a tree, on a warm, bright Sunday morning. And Lucas to shake her gently awake again. If that wasn't heaven, Thea didn't know what was.

She sat up on the cushions they'd slept on, straightened her T-shirt and ran her fingers through her hair, almost expecting to find it tumbling down her back, the way it once had.

'When did you cut your hair?' He was watching her thoughtfully.

'When I got back from Bangladesh. Do you hate it?'

'No. I hate the reason you cut it. I hate the reason that you wear grey all the time when red suits you better.'

'I wore red last night.'

'Yeah. Do you regret that?'

She knew what he was asking, and it wasn't about the dress. 'No. I don't regret one minute of last night.'

'Me neither.' He flopped back onto the cushions, surveying the branches above his head.

'What's that?' Lucas had changed his creased shirt for a T-shirt when he'd gone to make the coffee. She could see a thin blue line tracing out from under one of the sleeves.

He grinned. 'I indulged in a little body art. While you weren't looking.'

'How many?' Thea bit back the temptation to ask where. That might well turn into something she couldn't handle at the moment.

'Two. Both here.' He laid his hand on the top of his arm.

She breathed a sigh of relief. 'Well, what is it, then? An anchor? Sea serpents? Let's see it.'

He sat up and pulled at the sleeve of his T-shirt. 'That's really nice.' Thea didn't usually go for tattoos, but this one was tasteful and understated. A curved design, with roman numerals in the centre. She ran one finger across them and felt the muscle flex at her touch.

'Is that a date?'

'Fifteenth of May. It's Ava's birthday. When I first adopted her, she tested me, all the time. Wanted to know that I wasn't going anywhere. One of the things that she threw at me was that I'd forgotten her birthday the previous year and turned up with a present a week late. I promised I wouldn't do that again, but she said that was easy to say.'

'So you had her birthday tattooed on your arm.'

'Seemed like an idea at the time. Of course, I hadn't reckoned on her wanting one too. She was only seven.'

Thea choked with laughter. 'What did you say?'

'I said that tattoos were for adults. If she wanted one when she was eighteen...'

'You'd still say no.'

'Yeah. Something like that.'

'I think that's really sweet of you. Any girl would love a gesture like that. Where's the other one?'

He ran his finger across the top of the design, birds twisted together in flight, and Thea caught her breath. 'That part's separate?'

Lucas nodded, watching her face.

'They look like swifts.'

He grinned. 'Remember lying on our backs in that field in France, watching them fly?'

That had been when they'd had plans and dreams. When reaching for the freedom of the sky hadn't seemed impossible. 'I haven't thought about that in years.'

'It's a reminder. Of that time. Of you.'

She stared at him. On one level this was the sweetest, nicest gesture she could think of. On another it meant the ultimate sadness. There was a sort of finality about it, as if what they'd had only existed in a past that was locked away now. Something dead that could only be commemorated.

'What would you do if...?' Suddenly the thought of another woman seeing that tattoo made her want to cry. 'What happens if someone else sees it there?'

'Lots of people have seen it.' His gaze found hers and he gave up the pretence of not knowing what she was talking about. 'Not in the way you mean. Are you going to tell me to have it lasered off?'

'It would serve you right if I did.' She couldn't. Whatever it meant, it was still something that remained of a past that both hurt and was precious to her, and Thea couldn't bear to just rub it out. 'Keep it.'

He nodded, smiling as he rolled his sleeve back down. 'What are you doing today?'

'I thought I might go in to work at some point.'

'Stay. Ava's having lunch over at my parents' place today and I said I'd join them if I wasn't working. You're welcome to come along too.'

It was tempting. But tattoos and trees were one thing. At some point they had to get back to the real world. 'No. Thanks, but I really need to get going. I was going to go into work today, there are some things I need to catch up on.'

'Okay. Do you want a bit of company? I'll drop by my parents' place for a couple of hours and then come to the hospital. I can be there at twelve.'

'That would be good. Maybe we can work something out about any connections to this new case.' Slowly, word by word, the magic was dissolving. Like a night mist that couldn't withstand the sunshine.

'Yeah.' He lay on his back, still staring at the canopy above their heads. 'No need to move just yet, though.'

'No. Not just yet.'

Thea was at the hospital by eleven, checking through progress reports from the TB nurses and signing off treatment schedules. Half an hour later her phone rang, an unknown number coming up on the display.

'Thea Coleman.'

'Thea?'

'Ava? Is everything all right?' Thea hadn't given Ava her mobile number, but she supposed that Lucas might have. The thought occurred to her that maybe he wouldn't be coming, and she realised just how much she'd been looking forward to seeing him again.

'Yes. Can I talk to you?'

'Of course you can. What's on your mind?'

'I can't talk now. Lucas is on his way to the hospital, and he'll be there soon.'

'Do you want me to get him to call you when he gets here?'

'No. I want to ask *you* something. Can you meet me? It's important.'

A trickle of guilt crawled down Thea's spine. Had Ava seen her with Lucas that morning? 'Let's meet up for coffee in the place around the corner from your house. Would that suit you?'

'That would be great. In half an hour?'

'Half an hour's fine. I'll see you then, Ava.'

'Yeah, thanks. Don't tell Lucas, will you?' The call ended abruptly, as if Ava didn't want to hear any of the reasons that not telling Lucas might be a bad idea.

'Right.' Thea looked at her phone. Whether she liked it or not, she'd just agreed to meet up with Ava behind his back. To discuss an important matter of an unknown nature. Thea sighed, and scribbled a note for Lucas, leaving it on his desk.

An hour later, Thea walked back into the incident room at the hospital. Lucas was sitting at his desk, concentrating on something on the screen of his laptop.

'Lucas.'

His face broke into a smile when he saw her. Maybe it was waking up with him that morning that made that smile so much more potent. Or knowing that he had a tattoo. Or how his body felt when she lay next to it.

'Hi. Where have you been?'

'I had to go and meet someone.' Better get this over with. 'I met Ava for coffee, actually.'

'Ava? She didn't say anything about meeting you.'

'No, she called me after you left. She got my number from your phone. Apparently you should password it.'

'Clearly.' The penny dropped. 'So you and Ava have had a secret coffee assignation. Is this anything I'm supposed to worry about?'

'I don't think so. In fact, I think it's probably a very good thing.'

'So why are you being so vague?' The look he shot her was laden with suspicion.

'Because...' Thea dropped her car keys on her desk and sat down. 'Because she thinks you might not like what she had to say and I'm supposed to talk some sense into you.'

'Okay. That's making me feel better already. How were you thinking of talking some sense into me?'

'I'll work that one out if the need arises. It's really not that bad.'

'A minute ago it was *very good*. Tell me quickly before things deteriorate any further and it becomes a disaster.'

'Safiyah's got a boyfriend. He goes to the school around the corner. Ava thinks he may be the link we're looking for.'

'That's it?'

'The boyfriend hasn't been tested yet. Safiyah's tried to persuade him to come forward, but he won't because he doesn't want to get her into trouble.'

Lucas rolled his eyes. 'At least he's showing concern for Safiyah, however misguided. How does Ava know all this?'

'They all message each other. They've been chatting about it for days. Apparently a whole group of them got together and decided I was their best bet.'

'You?' There was a touch of hurt pride in his voice.

'Ava knows that I can put someone on the list for testing. She also knows that I'm a doctor and bound by professional confidentiality, so I can't just go to Safiyah's parents and tell them about her boyfriend.'

He thought for a moment. 'That's not entirely true. It's a bit of a grey area.' He frowned. 'Anyway, *I'm* a doctor. Couldn't she tell me?'

'And you're her parent. She reckons that's a conflict of interest for you. You said it yourself the other day.' Thea decided not to mention that Ava had said that Lucas would probably go ballistic if she told him.

'Right.' He thought for a moment. 'Actually, that's a pretty mature choice for her to have made.'

'I thought so.' Thea decided to change the subject while Lucas still seemed relatively happy with the situation. 'So how does that affect our thinking on the spread of the infection?'

He strode over to the white-board on the wall and started drawing circles. 'All right, so what do we know? There's Safiyah, and she's in contact with her boyfriend.' He frowned. 'Not too much contact, one hopes. Her mother's not going to like that one bit.'

He turned suddenly, weighing the marker pen in his hand. 'I don't suppose Ava happened to mention…'

'Whether she's got a boyfriend too? No, she didn't.'

'Couldn't you have asked? Woman to woman?'

'If she'd told me, woman to woman, that would imply I'm not supposed to tell anyone else.'

'Does it?' He gave her his most charming smile and Thea resisted it. 'You'd tell me if you'd discussed it, though?'

'What, so you could try to get me to tell you what we'd said?'

'Well, we both know that wouldn't work.'

No one even talked about Bangladesh, let alone joked about it. Thea drew in a startled breath and then found herself laughing. If Lucas had treated this like a dirty little secret, it would have compounded all her fears. Talking about it, laughing about it even, made it all shrink back into perspective.

'Yeah. Keep that in mind, eh?'

Lucas shrugged and returned to the white-board, drawing a few more circles. 'Okay, so we know that Derek Thompson's not our index case. What if Safiyah is? What if the infection passed to the boyfriend and then on to Derek?' He stood back and shook his head. 'No, that doesn't make sense.'

'Why not?'

'Because Derek's been ill for a while now. Safiyah would have been ill sooner.'

'Maybe her body fought the infection off for a while. Each case of TB develops at a different rate.'

'Yeah, sure. But she'd have had to be infectious for months. I don't see that much of her, Ava usually takes her over to my parents' for tea, but I think I'd have noticed if she had active pulmonary TB for the last six months.'

Thea nodded. 'True. Although if you're keeping a strict barrier between home and work, you probably shouldn't mention that...' A marker pen whizzed past her ear. 'Missed.'

'I meant to. Moving on...'

'Okay, moving on, it's the other way around. Derek passed the infection to the boyfriend who passed it on to Safiyah.'

'Maybe.' Lucas started to pace restlessly. 'Now there's something else I don't understand. In order to pass the infection on to Safiyah, he'd have to have active pulmonary TB. And yet if he's not been tested then he's not in any of the contact groups. And despite us briefing all the teachers on the symptoms to look out for, none of them have noticed. Does that sound very likely to you?'

'No.' Thea rested her chin on her hand. The problem seemed insoluble.

'We need to know more, and we need to know quickly.

There are a lot of kids at risk in those two schools.' He threw himself into his chair, rubbing his hand across his face. 'You do know this is killing me, don't you?'

It was a tough admission to make. Ava used to tell him everything, and now it seemed that he was the last to know. Even her friends thought that Thea was a more likely confidante than he was. He couldn't argue with the logic of that, but the reality of it was eating at him.

From the look on her face, Thea knew she was treading on eggshells. 'You're being very reasonable about it.'

He gave a snort of wry laughter. 'Yeah, well, looks can be deceptive.'

'It's a lot easier to discuss these things with someone you don't know so well. I wouldn't have talked about my friend's boyfriends to my dad.'

'Thanks.' That might be true, but it wasn't helping.

'At least we know to test the boyfriend now. If he is infected we have the chance to catch it early. And it might have been a little melodramatic, but Ava and her friends did the right thing.'

'I'll tell her that when I get home. In fact, I'll call her right now.'

Thea gifted him with a wonderful, glittering smile. 'I'll let you do that. I'm just going out to the drinks machine.'

Lucas found himself rubbing his arm, where the tattoo lay under his shirt, as he watched her go. He'd put it there as the one permanent reminder of the woman he'd loved and then lost through his own selfishness. Now it was different. A reminder that he hadn't just messed up his own life but hers as well. A reminder that he shouldn't do so again.

CHAPTER ELEVEN

Week Six

'How DID IT go with Ava last night?' Thea asked the question as soon as the Monday morning meeting was finished and they were sitting at their desks, facing each other.

Lucas shrugged. 'Oh, you know. She's a teenager. I'm apparently a fatal flaw in an otherwise pristine stratagem.'

'She said that?'

'Yeah. She's developing quite a line in carefully considered insults. I blame the debating society.'

Thea chuckled. 'Good girl. So which part of the pristine stratagem did you manage to disfigure?'

'Don't you start. Safiya told her that we were going to talk to her mother this morning. She thought that I might give the game away.'

'And I suppose you told Ava that it would look pretty fishy if we refused to talk to Safiyah's mother, let alone being completely unprofessional.'

'Yes, I did. Then I said that you'd undoubtedly rip my tongue out if I said a word out of place, and offered her ice cream.'

'And the ice cream worked?'

'Yep. I stopped off on the way home and got some Rocky Road.' Lucas grinned at her. 'I find that forward planning's the key.'

She returned his smile, and the room suddenly lit up. It did that every time. 'I prefer toffee fudge...'

'Yeah, I know you do.' The memory slammed him in the face. Toffee fudge ice cream, a hot day and Thea lying naked on his bed. Of all the times they'd eaten ice cream together, that had to have been the best. And probably the messiest.

He tried to put the memory back where it was supposed to be, somewhere in the portion of his brain that was not designed for access at random moments. Still it lingered faintly, like a cool summer breeze playing around his cerebral cortex.

'So are you ready to go?'

'In a minute.' She was tapping away at her computer keyboard. 'I've just got to quickly send my notes from the meeting off to Michael.'

Before she'd left the office, Thea had slung a bright silk scarf over her dark jacket, its indigo shades making her hair seem even more golden than usual. Lucas had complimented her on the way she looked and she'd blushed a little.

'Dr Coleman. Welcome to my home.' Safiya's mother opened the front door with a self-possessed smile.

'Thank you. And, please, call me Thea.'

'What a lovely name. Mine is Amina.' Amina led the way through to the sitting room and Thea sat down in the chair that she selected for her.

'What a beautiful room.'

Amina nodded in acknowledgement. When Lucas had visited briefly to collect Ava, he'd never seen this room anything other than spotless, unlike his own living room, which sometimes showed signs of wear and tear, produced by one teenager and one busy doctor.

They went through the preliminaries of tea, and Thea pronounced her delight at the home-made biscuits. She asked how Safiyah was, as if this were a social call, and nodded solicitously at Amina's answer. Then, as smooth as silk, she moved on to the business in hand.

'You have some concerns that you'd like to share with us.'

'I do.' Amina clasped her hands together in her lap. 'I have an idea where Safiyah may have caught TB.'

There was nothing on Thea's face, apart from polite interest. 'In terms of contact tracing, we promise absolute discretion.'

'That is not quite what I had in mind.' Amina smiled. 'I am worried for that person.'

This wasn't quite the way that Lucas had been expecting the conversation to go. At least Thea seemed to be keeping up and not showing the surprise that he felt.

'Amina, can you explain this to me a little more?'

Amina nodded. 'My sister's child has been unwell for some months now. The doctor said that it was a winter virus, and then that she had developed a slight case of pneumonia.'

'And she's no better now?'

'The doctor said that it would take a while to resolve. I told my sister that it was taking too long, but...' Amina shrugged. 'Mariam is still not fully recovered.'

'And she's not been referred to the hospital?' Maybe Lucas imagined the flicker of annoyance in Thea's face, it was so fleeting. She had every cause. There really was no excuse for a GP in central London not considering TB in this context.

'I urged her to insist. But she does not. She will do what the doctor tells her, over her own sister.'

'And Mariam and Safiyah are close? They see each other regularly?'

'Yes, they do.'

Thea smiled. 'Then we have no problem. Mariam will have to be tested for tuberculosis as part of the testing we'll need to do for all of Safiyah's contacts.'

'In ten weeks' time? She will have to wait that long?'

'No. Who told you ten weeks?' Lucas reckoned he knew the answer to that question.

Amina's gaze dropped to the carpet. 'Safiyah and your daughter have…they message each other. Safiyah told me.'

Thea grinned, and the tension that had suddenly filled the room wound back down again. 'Well, Ava's absolutely correct, we do normally wait, because ten weeks is the incubation period for the infection. But if someone is showing symptoms it's quite a different matter. I will do what's necessary to make sure that your niece is seen straight away.'

'Thank you.' Amina smiled. 'I appreciate that. My sister will do what is best for Mariam, but she may delay. The…shame.'

'There's no shame in any of this, Amina.'

'I know. Others don't think so. I had a call from one of the parents at school this morning. She was very apologetic but said that she was sure I would understand that it would not be appropriate for Safiya to come to her daughter's birthday party.'

'When's the party?' There was a trace of anger in Thea's tone.

'In six weeks' time.'

'Look, Amina, I haven't seen Safiyah and so I can't give an opinion on her particular case. But, in general, once a patient has been on the drug regime for two weeks, they're not infectious. When Safiyah's doctors give her the all-clear, it'll be perfectly all right for her to go to whatever party she wants to.' Thea was keeping her outrage under wraps. But it was there, like a hard backbone of truth in what she said.

'This is what they have told me.' Amina's mother shrugged miserably. 'But what can I do?'

Anger flashed in Lucas's heart. That well-worn organ, which had been jerked out of its enforced rest from the first moment he'd seen Thea again.

'You can help me, Amina. My daughter wants to see Safiyah, and I won't deny her the opportunity to see her friends because of someone's prejudice. As soon as Safiyah is non-infectious, I'd be grateful if you and your family would come to my house for a meal.'

'I...' Amina's self-control broke, and she looked suddenly flustered. 'I appreciate your offer, but the drugs make her sick.'

'I understand that. I'm a doctor, I can deal with that. What I can't deal with is irresponsible people who act out of prejudice. I won't deny my daughter the opportunity of seeing her friends just because someone who doesn't know the facts thinks it's a good idea.'

Amina straightened in her chair. 'No. This may cause Ava to become a talking point. I cannot allow it.'

He could feel Thea's gaze on him. Urging him to do what was right. 'One of the most valuable lessons I can teach my daughter is to stand up for her friends and to do what's right. It's not my place to deny her that and, respectfully, it's not yours either.'

He saw Thea's eyes widen. Had he done this for her? Or for Ava? The certain knowledge dawned on Lucas that he'd done this for himself. Because it was the right thing to do, and if he stood by and watched while another family was ostracised because of ignorance, he'd be as bad as the scaremongers. Worse, because he knew better.

Amina nodded slowly. 'I will convey your invitation to Safiyah.'

'I doubt that's necessary.' Lucas quirked his lips downwards. 'I imagine that Ava and Safiyah are already way ahead of us. I'd be surprised if the whole school doesn't know about it by now.'

Finally Amina laughed. 'Perhaps so. When the other parents see that you have made Safiyah your guest, they may change their minds.'

That had occurred to Lucas too. 'I hope so. When they

do it'll make my life easier in two areas. Professionally I need to spread the message that there's no stigma involved with TB.'

Thea chuckled. 'And personally he's got a teenage daughter.'

Amina laughed with her. 'Enough said.'

CHAPTER TWELVE

IT HAD BEEN a busy week again. Thea had called Mariam's doctor and he had co-operated completely. Mariam had been seen and was indeed suffering from active pulmonary tuberculosis. In one way it made things much clearer, since Mariam had spent the previous summer with her cousins in Birmingham, and Lucas had been able to confirm contact with one of the cases there. But how the infection had travelled six miles, from one school to another, was still a mystery.

He wasn't thinking about any of that at the moment, though. This was the one weekend of the year that had to be remembered. He and Ava usually went away with his parents to their cottage in Cornwall, but this time he'd stayed behind. The memories, which had become less painful over the years, weren't enough any more.

Sam's birthday. Exactly a week before Lucas's own, and when they'd been kids it had been the best week of the year. Now Lucas was sitting on a bench, opposite Sam's grave, thinking about how his big brother had taught him to ride his new bike.

Tears sprang to his eyes and Lucas went to wipe them away, even though there was no one there to see them. 'You were always there to pick me up. What am I going to do now?' Addressing his brother like this seemed a little weird, but it felt good.

The gravestone didn't answer. Of course it didn't. But somewhere in his head Lucas knew what the answer would be. *'Don't look at the ground, or you'll fall. Keep your eyes on where you want to go.'*

Lucas ventured another observation. 'I worry about Ava all the time. It's hard.'

The gravestone stared back at him blankly. Suddenly Lucas remembered something Sam had said just before he'd died. *'She's growing up. That's not supposed to be easy.'*

Lucas grinned. 'You and me both, eh, Sam?'

This was stupid. But he couldn't move away from this quiet place, surrounded by trees and flowers. And as he was there, he may as well give Sam the whole story.

'I'm working with Thea—you remember Thea. Ava loves her and she makes me want so much more out of life.'

He waited for an answer. Maybe here was none.

'You need to live your life, Lucas. We may not be breathing the same air, but we'll always be brothers.'

Sam's retort, when Lucas had first told him of his plans to go to Bangladesh and his fears that parting might change everything between them. It occurred to Lucas that this was the last place that Sam would have wanted to see him. That he wouldn't have wanted Lucas to put his own life on hold any longer.

'I hurt her, Sam.'

Nothing. Maybe he had to come up with the solution to that one all on his own. The one thing Lucas did know was that it was his responsibility to make sure that Thea wasn't hurt again.

He wiped the tears from his face. He should go, before someone found him here, talking to ghosts and voices in his head. But he couldn't move. And if someone found him crying, who cared? This was between him and his brother.

Two hours later, Lucas said his farewells to Sam and Claire and walked away. He supposed that he should feel better, but he wasn't quite sure how he felt. Lighter, perhaps. It was difficult to tell. Maybe it was just the sunshine and the quietness, which had cleared his mind a little.

He got into his car and stared at his phone. Without consciously making a decision about what he was going to do next, he dialled.

'What's up?'

'I'm hungry. Do you want some lunch?'

A pause. 'What's going on, Lucas?'

'Nothing.' Everything. 'It's Sam's birthday today.'

'I remember. A week before yours. You want to talk about something?'

She remembered his birthday. The thought made Lucas smile. 'No, I don't want to talk about anything. I want to have lunch with you.'

Another pause. 'What about Ava?'

'She's in Cornwall with my parents. I stayed behind.' An idea occurred to him and Lucas found himself grinning into his phone. 'I could murder a plate of oysters.'

He heard her laugh quietly. 'Okay, then. Oysters it is.'

He was parked outside her flat, leaning against the car. Lucas knew she'd be watching for him, and Thea knew in return that he didn't have a trip to a restaurant in mind. His worn-out jeans and beach shoes confirmed it.

He eyed the towel poking out of the top of her canvas bag. 'So much for trying to surprise you.'

'You surprised me when you called. And you can't go to the beach without paddling.'

She handed her bag to him. That was all it took to slip back into the easy etiquette of a couple. He stowed it in the back of the car and opened the passenger door for her.

'Music or wind?' Lucas grinned as she got into his car.

'You know I want music. But as you've got a convertible now...'

He shrugged. 'I can't think why. I don't think I've ever driven around with the top down.'

'What?' She gave him a reproving look. 'Okay, let's have music on the motorway, and when we see the sea, we'll put the top down.'

'Sounds like a plan.' He slid a CD into the player and fiddled with the volume.

'What's this?' She didn't recognise the song.

'One of Ava's. We play one track each and this one's hers. Skip on to the next one if you like.'

'No, let's have Ava's as well.' She settled into her seat. 'So where exactly are we going?'

Lucas gave her a melting smile. 'Take a guess…'

An hour on the motorway and then branching off into Kent was the first clue. They made Whitstable in just over two hours, and it wasn't long enough for Thea. She could have driven all afternoon with him, favourite tracks on the CD player just begging to be sung along with and the road stretching out in front of them.

'Aha.' She straightened in her seat. 'Look, look I see the sea. Over there.'

'Where?'

'You missed it. It was there, definitely.'

'Okay.' He slowed down, pulling into a lay-by and turning the car around.

'What? Don't you believe me?'

'Just checking.' He leaned across to see out of the passenger window. Quite unnecessary really, but it seemed essential right now. 'That's not the sea. It's mist.'

'Yeah, mist over the sea. Put the top down.'

Lucas shrugged and operated the control for the automatic roof of the car. 'Happy?'

'Very.'

'You want to put your scarf over your head?' He indicated the bright scarf that she had wrapped around her shoulders.

'No, I want to feel the wind in my hair.' It might be short, but it was still hair. And this was the seaside.

They drove down towards the sea, stopping outside a couple of seafood restaurants on the way. Both were fully booked. Fate seemed to be driving them down towards the water, and Lucas finally managed to get them a small table in the open air at a restaurant close to the beach.

'You first.' He inspected the dozen oysters that lay on a bed of crushed ice in front of them and indicated the plumpest.

'I like that one, for starters.' Thea indicated another, smaller specimen. 'I'll work my way up.'

He chuckled, lacing the oyster with a few drops of juice from a quarter of lemon, just the way she liked it. Thea reached for the delicacy, but he had already picked it up.

'Ready?' His lips quirked into a smile.

'Go for it.'

He put the flat edge of the shell to her lips and tipped. The oyster slid into her mouth, without spilling a drop of the juice.

'Mmm.' She chewed once, and the taste of the sea filled her mouth. Then sweetness on her tongue. 'These are very good. Try one.'

He picked out one for himself and downed it. 'They are, aren't they? Maybe we should have had two dozen.'

'Too rich. I haven't eaten oysters in ages. I'd have to work myself up to having a whole dozen of them.'

He nodded. 'Yeah. Baby steps to start with, eh?' Lucas looked up as the waiter approached with an ice bucket and expertly wrested the cork from a bottle of champage without anything more than a demure pop.

'More champagne?' Thea grinned at him. 'What are you trying to do, prop up the industry?'

'I reckoned on a toast. Seeing that it's Sam's birthday today and mine in a week's time.'

He was smiling. That strained look whenever he talked about Sam seemed to have blown away on the wind.

'That's a great idea. Down in one, and then smash the glasses.' She looked at the two, mass-produced glasses that the waiter had brought, wondering if she dared.

Lucas laughed. 'Do you know why they smash glasses after a toast?'

'No. Why?' Thea had always thought it had an air of finality about it.

'It's a way of making sure that the glass can never again be used to drink a toast to someone else, who may be less important.' He took the bottle from the ice bucket, pouring a little into each of their glasses, the foam fizzing up.

'Mmm. I like that.' She squeezed a little lemon juice onto two oysters, handing him one. 'Oysters, and then you make the toast.'

'Down in one?'

'Absolutely.' She grinned at him. That was the way that she and Lucas had always done things. Never by halves.

They swallowed the oysters and then Lucas held his glass towards hers. 'To Sam and Claire. Happy birthday, Sam.'

A tear glistened at the corner of his eye, but he was smiling. Thea tipped her glass against his.

'Sam and Claire.'

She drank, and bubbles rushed up her nose. 'Oh. That's good stuff.'

'What, you want me to get a cheap bottle for Sam and Claire?'

It really didn't matter. They could have drunk the toast in cold tea and it would have meant the same. It was the change that had been wrought in Lucas's heart that mattered. The way he seemed to be celebrating his brother's life, instead of thinking only of his death.

'You should do this every year. Go somewhere and drink a toast.'

He shrugged. 'Perhaps I will.' His gaze caught hers and held it. 'Maybe it just needed to be done the once.'

'Then let's do it right.' Thea tightened her fingers around the slender stem of the glass, snapping it in two.

He gave a small nod, snapping the stem of his own glass and putting the pieces onto a napkin. 'Sam would have said this was a terrible waste. He was always the practical one.' A tiny trickle of blood ran over Lucas's trembling fingers and he brushed it away.

'No, he wouldn't. You said that he used to look after his little brother.'

'Yes, he did.'

Lucas turned to the waiter, who had hurried over and was looking questioningly at the two broken glasses on the table. He pulled a note from his wallet, which covered the cost of the glasses plus a generous tip, and the waiter didn't ask, just gathered up the pieces in a napkin.

'I'll bring another two glasses, sir.'

'No. Do you have a couple of paper cups so we can take this away and drink it on the beach?'

'You can't drink champagne out of paper cups.' The waiter looked mildly affronted. Clearly he didn't know Lucas. 'I'll bring another couple of glasses and you can take them with you. This'll cover it.'

They had picked their way across the smooth, sun-baked pebbles on the beach and found a spot out of the wind by one of the heavy wooden groynes that ran down the beach and into the sea. Lucas poured a full glass of champagne for Thea and a half for himself.

'Hey, what are you trying to do, get me drunk?'

'I'm driving.' He grinned. 'Getting you drunk is just a side agenda.'

She flopped back onto the warm shingle. 'I'll go and get some orange juice later to dilute it.'

He chuckled. 'That doesn't make any difference. And how many more ways can you think of to ruin good champagne?'

'Hundreds...possibly thousands.' Thea stared up at the clear blue sky. This was heaven. 'So what are you doing for your birthday?'

'Dunno. You'll keep the evening free?'

'If you like.' The invitation was very casual, and her answer was equally offhand. But then Lucas touched the cold champagne bottle to the top of her arm, making her shiver. He could turn the smallest gesture into an act of slow, melting seduction.

'You're sure you know the date?'

'I know it. Tenth of July. Eighteen hundred hours.'

'You know what time I was born? I don't even know that.'

'Six o'clock is when we get off work. You were probably born at two in the morning, but I'm not going to wake up and sing "Happy Birthday" to you then.' Thea adjusted the concept. It was almost second nature now to believe that they must be sleeping together, even though they'd barely touched today. 'You probably wouldn't answer your phone, anyway.'

He chuckled. 'I'll put it on vibrate and tape it over my heart.'

CHAPTER THIRTEEN

THEY STAYED ON the beach until the sun began to graze the horizon, then wandered back up to the car, stowing the half-drunk bottle in the footwell in the hope that it might retain some of its fizz after they got home, and putting the two glasses back on an empty table outside the restaurant. Lucas got chips from a fish and chip shop a couple of doors along, and they walked back to the beach to eat them.

'Mayonnaise. You remembered.' Thea dunked one of her chips in the tub of home-made mayonnaise that Lucas had bought for her.

'Yeah. I remember all your bizarre culinary preferences.' He dunked his own chip into a similar tub of tomato sauce.

'What, chips and mayonnaise? Nothing wrong with that is there? Try some.'

'Nah. Not after oysters.' He flopped onto his back on the sun-warmed shingle, leaving Thea to stare out across the bay.

'Can I ask you something?' The question had been bugging her since he'd first called that morning. 'Seriously?'

'Yeah, of course.'

'What are we doing here?'

Lucas took a while to mull over the answer. 'I reckon we've known each other too long to be acquaintances. We're either friends or enemies, and I really want it to be friends.'

So did she. 'Okay. Friends is good.'

They finished their chips and strolled back down towards the sea again, taking off their shoes and leaving them on the thick posts of one of the wooden groynes. Thea rolled up her trouser legs, picking her way over the sand and stones and into the water.

'How is it?'

'Lovely and cool. It's a bit squishy, though. I'm sinking into the sand.'

'Well, don't stay in one place for too long. You might get sucked under and then I'd have to explain to Michael Freeman how I managed to lose his best doctor.'

'Hah! So you wouldn't come in and rescue me?' Thea threw down the challenge.

'Nah, I don't want to get wet. Hey!' He dodged to one side as Thea splashed some water towards him. 'Watch out.'

He bent, rolling up the legs of his jeans as far as they would go. Thea picked her way further into the sea, and he splashed after her. The gentle incline of the beach meant that by the time he caught her they were still only standing in six inches of water.

'You want to get me wet, eh?' He swept her off her feet and into his arms, bending over as if he was going to dunk her into the water and then straightening up at the last moment.

'No!' Telling him he wouldn't dare would only make him do it. She wound her arms tightly around his neck and gave him a pleading look. 'Don't…'

'Say it nicely.'

'Please.'

'Nicer than that.'

She leaned in to him, her lips grazing his cheek as she spoke. 'Please.' She planted a kiss behind his ear, and felt him shudder.

Slowly he let her down, and she felt her feet touch the

water. She kept her arms around his neck, as if losing contact with him now would be letting him go for ever.

He kissed the top of her head. 'I think…'

'Don't think, Lucas.'

When she tipped her face up towards him, Lucas almost lost his balance in the water. Her pale skin was almost ethereal in the setting sun and her eyes…her eyes were like the soft lights of home, glimmering out into the dusk.

She didn't hesitate but she didn't rush things either. Her lips met his, just when he thought he couldn't stand it any longer, and broke away just at the right moment. It wasn't quite what Lucas had been thinking when he'd said 'friends' but he couldn't help it.

'Not good enough.' She stood on her toes to murmur in his ear.

'I'll admit I'm a bit rusty.'

'No, you're not.' She brushed her lips against his again, and he felt a shudder run through him. 'But it would be so much better if you used your hands. And if you didn't treat me as if I'm made of glass.'

He chuckled, resting his fingers lightly on her waist. She planted a kiss on his cheek and Lucas pulled her in hard, stifling her gasp with his mouth. Sliding one hand up her back, he hooked it over her shoulder, pinning her against him. He'd wanted this for so long.

Then the synchronicity. It was so startling it almost knocked him off his feet. As if she'd suddenly given up any pretence of being separate from him, and her heart was beating in time with his. Every breath he took was matched by one of hers. Every touch had an equal and opposite reaction. He had to let her go now, before he lost control and pulled her down into the water.

He let her down slowly so that she was in no doubt about the fact that he really didn't want to. Gently pulled his aching body away from hers, knowing that he'd left a part of him behind. The part that had always belonged to Thea.

'What shall we toast this time?' She brushed her lips against his in an action that affirmed everything that was good in his life.

'Things we've lost. Things we've found.'

She smiled. 'Yeah. Things we've lost. And found.'

Their kiss was tender this time. No more desperately trying to forget the past and not think about the future. Just this moment.

They both knew the exact time to end it, and she nestled against him, her fingers resting lightly on his hips. No trying to claw it back, no trying to repeat it. It had been perfect, just as it was.

Finally, she took a step backwards, yelping suddenly as she trod on something in the water. Standing on one foot, she tried to inspect the sole of the other, laughing as she swayed precariously. Lucas reached out to steady her, but she'd already lost her balance and she fell backwards.

'Ow-w-w.' She obviously wasn't hurt as she was still laughing and Lucas held out his hand, helping her to her feet. Turning around, she inspected the back of her trousers, caked now with sand and mud. 'D'you reckon I could be any dirtier?'

He inspected the back of her trousers. 'Nope. You could be a bit wetter, though. Look, you've missed a bit, just there.'

'Don't you dare.' She threw him a menacing look, and Lucas resisted the temptation to splash water on her blouse. 'We'll walk a bit. It'll dry off.'

They'd have to walk a long way—she was soaked. 'I have a towel in the car.'

Thankfully, it was a large one. Standing next to the car, Thea wound the towel around her waist, tucking it in firmly, and slipped her trousers off. They were soaking, and when she wrung them out a puddle of dirty water formed on the pavement.

'Time to go home?' He was leaning against the bonnet of the car, watching her.

'Guess so.' Thea slid into the front seat and arranged the towel over her legs.

The soundtrack for the way back was slower, moody late-night songs. The headlights of the oncoming cars were almost mesmeric, and Thea began to doze.

Her eyes snapped open. The heat in the car was suddenly unbearable and when she found the button to wind down the window, the wind that hit her in the face was worse. 'Pull over... Going to be sick...'

She had no idea where they were, but the sudden deceleration told her that they must be on the motorway. Hard shoulder. Blurred light flashing in her eyes. She had to get out...

As she instinctively reached for the door release, she heard the central locking click. Her stomach cramped suddenly and she doubled over. Not yet. Can't be sick in the car. She clamped her hand over her mouth.

'Let it go, Thea. You'll choke yourself.' Lucas's voice, cool and steady.

'Stop the damn car,' She groaned as her stomach lurched again. The car finally came to a halt, and she heard the locks release.

By the time Lucas made it around to her door, she'd managed to get it open and had almost fallen out of the car and onto the tarmac. He half carried her onto the grass by the side of the hard shoulder and she fell to her knees, throwing up almost immediately.

'Okay. That all of it?'

Thea was shaking too much to answer. Her stomach started to twist into knots again and she felt her back spasm painfully as she retched violently.

The sharp smell of her own vomit hit her. Sweat and

tears were trickling down her face, and she was suddenly
cold. She felt Lucas move her, sitting her down on something, and she sagged to one side, leaning against a fence.

'Stay there…just for a minute while I get you some
water.'

'Yeah. Sorry.' The indignity of it all was sinking in fast.
On her hands and knees, wearing a towel, being sick by
the side of the road. Things rarely got much more humiliating than that.

'Here.' He handed her a bottle of water, steadying her
hand as she almost sploshed it all over her. 'Wash your
mouth out and then drink some.'

She obeyed him automatically. 'Sorry.'

'Be quiet.'

'But I am,' Thea protested weakly, and he wrapped his
arm around her shoulder.

'Stop it. How are you feeling now?'

'Better. I just want to lie down for a while.' Suddenly
curling up on the grass and sleeping didn't seem like such
a terrible idea.

'Yeah, I know. Sit in the car for a moment and rest. Then
we'll get you home.'

He had to stop again so that her aching stomach could reject
the water she'd drunk. When the car finally drew to a halt
for the third time she neither knew nor cared where she
was, just that he'd carried her out of the car and laid her
down on cool sheets. She slept for what seemed like five
minutes and then the convulsive retching started again,
this time all the more painful because of the stretched and
aching muscles in her back and stomach.

Lucas was there when she woke. The curtains were closed
and blowing slightly in the breeze, and she was in her own
bed. She was very thirsty.

'Hey, there.' He'd carried a chair from the living room

into her bedroom and was sitting in the corner of the room. 'How are you feeling?'

Terrible. She felt awful. Memories of last night started to filter back into her consciousness, fitting themselves back together like a jigsaw puzzle.

'Can I have some water, please?' Anything to get him out of the room for a moment while she gathered her scattered wits.

'Yes, of course.'

She heard the sound of his footsteps on the stairs and looked around. From the violence with which she'd been sick last night, she expected to see the room in complete disarray, but everything was just as it always was. The fresh smell of clean sheets drifted into her consciousness, and she remembered that Lucas had changed them at some point last night.

'Here.' He sat down on the edge of the bed and Thea slowly pulled herself up on the pillows and took the glass from his hand, drinking greedily. 'Slowly now. Not too much.'

'That's better. Thanks.' She handed the glass back to him.

Something wasn't right. Last night should have been one of the most humiliating of her life, but somehow it hadn't been. She could remember waking up, trying to get out of bed and falling flat on her face, then Lucas scooping her up and taking her to the bathroom. When it was all over he'd been as businesslike as the most practised of nurses, stripping off her soiled nightie, washing her and re-dressing her and putting her back to bed.

She felt herself redden a little at the thought. 'Ohh. I'm so sorry, Lucas.'

He shrugged. 'Nothing to apologise for.'

'There must be.' She couldn't remember quite what it was but she'd think of something. 'What's the matter with me? The oysters?'

'I ate the oysters too. Anyway, they're all irradiated these days. What did you have to eat yesterday morning?'

'Black coffee. Toast.' Not the most obvious candidates for food poisoning. Thea concentrated on remembering everything she'd eaten yesterday, her stomach growling in protest at even the thought of food. 'Mayonnaise. You didn't have any of that, and it was home-made.'

He nodded. 'Sounds as if that's what it is, then.'

'Or a bug of some sort.' Even thinking was tiring her out. Thea slumped against the pillows.

'I don't think so. I called the hospital this morning to see if there had been any reports of sickness amongst the staff or patients, and there's nothing. And you had no fever or any other symptoms.'

That was good to know. 'Apart from feeling as if I wanted to die, that is.'

He chuckled. 'Yeah. Apart from that.'

Then she remembered. The feel of his body next to her, lying on top of the bed. Holding her. Comforting her. How his being there had made all the difference.

'Thanks for sticking with me. I really appreciate it.'

'That's what friends are for.' His gaze dropped from her face, and he seemed to be examining a spot in the far corner of the room.

She'd said something but she couldn't remember what. She could see it in his face. 'What did I say, Lucas?'

'You said you felt terrible.' He shot her a grin. 'To someone with my medical training, that was relatively obvious.'

He was deflecting the question. There was something. Then she remembered. 'Oh, no. Lucas, I'm sorry… I didn't mean it, I was sick.'

His gaze met hers. 'You were right.'

'You couldn't have known. How could you have been there?' She'd woken in the night, after dreaming of the darkness of the Bangladeshi police cell. And she'd cried, asking Lucas why he hadn't come to fetch her. Why he hadn't been there.

'I just wish I had been.' He reached forward, brushing her hair from her brow in a motion of exquisite tenderness. 'You need to rest. I'll bring you some more water.'

'Wait.' She caught hold of his arm. 'I'm so sorry, Lucas.'

'Hey, stop that.'

'No, really. You've looked after me and all I did was give you a hard time.'

A grin crept over his face. 'Not exactly.'

'What?' She knew that look. 'What else did I say?'

'When I got you into the shower and switched the water on, you must have thought we were still on our way home because you gave a great big sigh and told me it was raining now, and that was all you needed.'

That wasn't so bad. She remembered him putting her back into bed, and that she'd felt clean and cared for. Safe...

Oh, no. Had she dreamed it, or had she actually said it?

'Nothing else?' I love you? Maybe she had just thought the words and never managed to say them.

He shook his head slowly. 'No.' He picked up the empty glass from the bedside. 'You were muttering a bit but I didn't catch any of it. I'll get you some more water.'

'Thanks.' She wasn't going to admit to saying it, and Lucas wouldn't admit to hearing it. Thea wondered whether that meant that it really had never been said. She leaned back against the pillows, too tired to think about anything any more. Just that Lucas had got her through the night.

CHAPTER FOURTEEN

Week Nine

LUCAS'S BIRTHDAY CELEBRATION was delayed by a week so that Safiya and her family could come. Thea arrived half an hour early, wearing a powder-blue dress, which complemented her hair and skin perfectly.

'You're early.' She looked gorgeous.

She smiled, and his heart started to beat faster. 'I have something for you.'

'Come in.' He stepped back from the doorway. Ava had already gone over to her grandparents' to help prepare lunch, and he was alone in the house.

She was holding a package, wrapped up in bright paper. Whatever it was paled into insignificance in comparison to thirty minutes alone with her before they were expected at his parents' house.

'Would you like something to drink? Ava's been experimenting with fruit punch.' He walked through to the kitchen and opened the fridge door and she giggled delightedly. 'Yeah, okay. She did quite a lot of experimenting.'

'And which ones of these are yours?' She surveyed the line of glasses, each topped with foil and each of them containing a different combination of fruit juices.

'Since Ava's not here, I'm blaming her for all of them. Although I'm quite pleased with that one.'

'It's separating out.'

'Yeah. Rather a nice rainbow effect, I thought.' He grinned at her and she chose a glass of green juice. 'That's one of Ava's.'

She sniffed at it delicately. 'Smells interesting.'

'You're quite sure?' Clearly Thea was braver than he was.

She took a sip and nodded. 'Yeah. Not bad. Tastes as if it's probably quite good for you.'

'I'll give it a miss, then.' Lucas reached for a yellowish concoction that he knew to be mainly orange juice. 'Here.' He produced a red and white striped drinking straw from the cupboard, along with a yellow cocktail umbrella, and arranged them in her glass. If that combination of colours didn't put her off, nothing would.

'Thank you. Got any cherries?'

'No. Good grief, you're worse than Ava.'

She grinned at him. 'You say the nicest things.'

Turning, she walked into the sitting room. Lucas followed her. Three minutes in to the thirty and he was already entranced.

'So.' She sat down on the sofa next to him, putting the package down on the coffee table. 'Are you going to open it now or do you want to guess what's inside?'

'Hmm. Round and flat.' Lucas tried to think of something that was that approximate shape. 'Can I pick it up?'

'No.'

Lucas stared at the package. 'Could *you* pick it up and shake it? Just so I can hear whether it rattles or not.'

'No.'

'It's…' He shrugged. 'A collapsible top hat.'

She laughed, and he felt a little thrill of pleasure. 'No. It might have been if I'd thought of that, though.'

'A…' Lucas gave up the unequal struggle and leaned back in his chair. 'Okay, you've got me. I don't know what it is.'

She gave a little nod, as if to accept his surrender. 'In that case, you can open it.'

She sat watching him, grinning when he got to the circular gift box, which contained another, square package. Smiling with delight when he smiled. 'That's... Thea, that's fantastic.'

She hadn't spent a lot of money, but it must have taken her a great deal of time and effort to find this. A beautifully tooled Victorian volume, the name of the former owner inscribed carefully inside the front cover and Thea's own inscription below that, as if it were part of an ongoing record of the book's travels. It was one of his favourite authors, and the book itself was in beautiful condition.

'I'm glad you like it.'

Lucas chuckled. 'You knew I'd love it.'

She laughed happily. 'It's good to keep an element of doubt. It makes giving presents more fun.'

'Thank you.' He leaned towards her, kissing her cheek. Just a brush of the lips, but he heard her catch her breath. Felt his own senses lurch into overdrive, revelling in her scent and the soft touch of her skin.

'You're welcome.' A slight flush rose in her cheeks.

'I suppose we should go over for lunch now.' He didn't want to. But twenty more minutes might be more of a temptation than he could bear.

'Yeah. Suppose we should.'

Neither of them moved. The warmth of the shared silence was intoxicating. Even if he couldn't touch her, he and Thea had always done silence well. Sitting, sharing random thoughts and observations. Watching the world go by in the undemanding security of each other's company.

When the clock on the mantelpiece chimed the hour, they hurried together across the lawn, arriving at the back of his parents' house at approximately the same time as Safiya and her parents arrived at the front. Ava greeted Safiya with a hug, and his mother served lunch in the large conservatory.

The initial polite conversation quickly gave way to genuine warmth between the families. When Safiya began to tire, she was despatched upstairs to lie down in the spare room, and coffee was served on the lawn.

'How is Mariam?' Thea asked Amina.

'She is improving. She has been very upset that she was falling behind with her studies.' Amina smiled. 'Safiya does not have this problem. But keeping Mariam away from the library is difficult. She spends a great deal of time there.'

Thea shot him a look, one eyebrow arched in query. Lucas nodded. He knew about this already, and was in the process of liaising with the local hospital.

'Safiya tells me that you are going to France for three weeks.' Amina turned to Ava. 'You must be looking forward to it.'

'Yes, but I'll be able to message Safiya. When we get back, Lucas and Thea are going to Mumbai, but that's for work. Thea's giving a talk at a conference.'

'My first. I'm dreading it.' Thea gave a little smile, as if the dread wasn't all that bad. Lucas knew that wasn't true, but at least she was talking about it. He hadn't heard her mention it to anyone else before now.

'Oh, I'm sure you'll be wonderful.' Amina looked at her husband and he nodded in agreement. 'It won't be too hot in September. Maybe a little wet.'

'I used to love staying inside and drinking tea at monsoon time. Watching the rain.'

Lucas caught his breath. It was just a memory. But it had broken through the barrier of misery that seemed to separate Thea from the world. Maybe, in time, there would be more like this.

'This isn't your first time in Asia?' His father looked

puzzled and Lucas glared at him, willing him to leave well alone.

'I lived in Bangladesh for two years. I was working at a TB clinic.'

'That must have been very challenging.' The hairs on the back of his neck prickled as Amina spoke again.

'In more ways than I could have imagined. I loved it there, though.' Thea looked almost as if she couldn't believe what she was saying, but she shot him a grin and Lucas relaxed.

'I hope that you return, then.'

'Thank you. I hope so too.' There was a touch of defiance in Thea's eyes. She might be afraid, and uncertain, but she was fighting back now.

His father waited until that evening, when everyone had gone, to ask. Lucas had known for some time that the question was coming.

'I didn't realise that Thea had gone to Bangladesh.'

'No. Neither did I until about a month ago.'

His father nodded thoughtfully. 'Anything to do with you?'

Lucas sighed. He'd resolved that if Thea could talk about it then so could he, but it still wasn't easy. 'Yeah, I think so. She had a bad time and I wasn't there to help her.'

His father walked over to the sideboard, picking up the brandy decanter and pouring a measure into two glasses. Something about his demeanour reminded Lucas of all the times he'd measured ice cream into a bowl for Ava. 'What sort of bad time?'

Lucas took the brandy and swirled it in the glass. 'Thea helped a fifteen-year-old girl who was pregnant and had been beaten by her husband. And instead of giving her a medal for that, the police locked her up on a trumped-up kidnapping charge.'

'How long did they hold her for?'

'Two weeks. Thea wouldn't say where the girl was, even when they threatened her with a long prison sentence.'

'Brave girl.' His father took a mouthful of brandy, seeming to decide that the details could wait until another time. 'I always liked Thea. Never understood why you two didn't get married.'

'Things happened, Dad. You know that.'

'Life goes on as well.'

'I was the one at fault when we broke up and she suffered for it. I won't do that to her again.'

'Then don't.'

'I don't intend to.' His father had much too high an opinion of him. Lucas didn't trust himself around Thea. He'd messed up once, and the best way to avoid doing so again was to let her be.

Week Ten

Just as she was about to leave work, Thea's mobile rang. 'Where are you?'

She raised her eyebrows at the peremptory question. 'At the hospital. Why?'

'Good. I'll be there in fifteen minutes to pick you up. See you then?' It sounded as if Lucas was in his car.

'Yes, if you like.'

'Great.' The call was abruptly cut off.

Maybe he'd just driven into a black spot. Or maybe that was all he'd had to say for himself. Thea had hardly seen Lucas all week. She'd been busy and his involvement at the hospital was dwindling anyway. There were other cases, other people that needed his time.

She decided to wait for him at the main gate and sent off a text to let him know. Almost exactly fifteen minutes later, his car swung into the entrance, and she saw him.

Why did she have to smile like that? Thea had been coming to terms with the fact that Lucas wasn't a permanent fixture in her life. They'd been thrown together by work, a red dress and a young woman named Safiya. On a day-to-day basis, Lucas had other things on his mind.

'What's up?' She got into the car next to him.

'I think we've got our source.' He swung the car around and drove back the way he'd just come.

'Really? Who?'

'It's not a who. It's a where.' He grinned smugly.

'And we're going to the where. Wherever that happens to be.'

'If I'm right, it'll make an interesting addition to your paper. And don't you want to be in on it if this turns out to be what wraps up the whole investigation?'

The end of their work together. Suddenly the trip to the conference in India seemed like a good thing. While it was still in her future, there was still a reason to look forward to seeing him again.

'Okay. This isn't a quiz show. You don't need to keep the suspense up.'

He chuckled. 'Don't you love it?'

'No, I don't.'

He shrugged. 'We're going to the library. I've got a hunch that it's where Derek Thompson came into contact with Mariam.'

'They both used the same library? Even if they did meet there somehow, it's not really enough exposure to pass a TB infection on.'

'Well, the library is in the same building as an amateur theatre. And before Christmas Mariam spent a lot of time there in the evenings, revising for her mock exams. Derek Thompson was in the storeroom at the theatre, painting scenery.'

'Is that all you've got? That they were in the same building at the same time. That doesn't even resemble contact.'

'But there are common services to both the theatre and the library. Heating, water, *ventilation*…'

'It's not going to travel through the ventilation system. Good ventilation disperses airborne particles and decreases the risk of infection.'

'Yeah, but this is an old building. There have been a number of cases where airborne infections have travelled through faulty ventilation systems. And I contacted the local authority, and it seems that they don't have any documents for the annual check last year. Which means it probably wasn't carried out.'

He drummed his fingers against the steering-wheel as he waited for the traffic lights to change. 'Look, I know it's circumstantial, but it's worth a look, isn't it? I've got a feeling...'

One of Lucas's feelings. Perhaps he was on the right track. 'It does fit in with everything that we know.'

'Exactly.' He accelerated away from the lights as soon as they turned green. 'The more I thought about it, the more I reckoned you were exactly right. That somehow Derek Thompson had some direct contact with Mariam. And this is the only thing I can come up with.'

He'd been thinking about her. Not *about her* exactly, but she'd had some part of his thoughts. And Thea could never resist Lucas's enthusiasm. 'Okay, then. Let's have a look.'

The library was closed on Wednesday evenings but a caretaker, who was obviously expecting Lucas, let them in.

'You have a separate quiet room.'

'Over here.' The caretaker marched them towards a high, panelled door.

'You keep this door closed in the winter?'

'Yes, mostly. It gets too cold in there otherwise to sit for very long. Are we in trouble here?'

Lucas shook his head. 'Not as far as I know. We just need to know what happened.' He walked into the study room and smiled. 'See that? Mariam says that she always

sat in the same seat, over there.' He pointed to a large polished wood table, which stood beneath a ventilation grille.

'So far so good for your theory. Let's go and see the
other end of it.'

Lucas had left her in the messy back room of the theatre,
which was stacked high with painted scenery boards and
boxes of props. Her phone rang.

'Nothing yet.' She sniffed the air.

'I've only just lit the incense sticks. When I closed the
door, the smoke went straight up towards the ventilator.'

'I don't smell anything.' Thea sniffed the air. Maybe...
'Patchouli!'

Lucas's delighted chuckle reached down the phone.
'Right in one!'

By the time he'd navigated the maze of corridors that led
from the library to the props room, the smell of patchouli
hung heavy in the air.

'Good grief. There's no mistaking it, is there?' He
looked speculatively up at the ventilation grille in the wall.

'Looks as if you were right.' Thea grinned up at him.

'Only because you were.' He returned the smile. 'I've
got the master keys from the caretaker. Let's see where
else we can smell it.'

They toured the library and the theatre together, opening doors and trying to catch the unmistakeable scent. The
library was completely clear, unless you stood right by the
door of the study room, and so was the theatre, apart from
a couple of box rooms adjoining the props room.

'At least there's nothing in here.' Lucas had switched on
the lights in the auditorium of the theatre and they mean-
dered down past the seating to the foot of the stage. 'That
was what was worrying me most. Derek's wife said there
was a kids' pantomime on here before Christmas.'

The thought made Thea shudder. 'You'll need to do
some further testing of the system, though, surely?'

'Yes, we will. I'll be commissioning an urgent inspection first thing in the morning. But this is a first indication.' He climbed up onto the stage and Thea gave a round of applause from the auditorium. Lucas bowed deeply.

'I reckon if I go up into the loft…I bet I can work it out if I can see the ducting for the ventilation.'

'It's probably filthy up there. And you don't know anything about ventilation systems.'

'Don't you want to know?'

'We do know. The patchouli went straight to the props room from where Mariam was sitting.'

'Yes, but we don't know how.'

Thea rolled her eyes. 'Come on, then. If you're going up there, I'm coming too. You need someone to keep you out of trouble.'

It seemed that he'd come prepared, because he had torches, face masks and heavy-duty gloves in the boot of his car. They found the caretaker, who showed them through to some back steps that led up to the roof area, and unlocked the door at the top for them.

'No one ever comes up here. Not since we had a problem with the water tank two years ago.'

'That's good to know.' Lucas handed a mask to Thea and walked into the loft area.

It was hot up there, and the air smelled musty. Lucas shone the beam of his torch along the ventilation ducts, which criss-crossed the space.

'I can't see anything wrong with these. And I don't smell any patchouli.'

They walked carefully across the boarded floor, looking for any signs of something that was out of place.

'Nothing.' Thea was suddenly disappointed. Someone else would find the final clue that they'd been searching for all these weeks.

'There must be more than this.' Lucas checked the plans

of the building. 'Yeah, look. The loft's divided into two sections. This part we're in here is over the library, and there's a second half over the theatre.'

They found a doorway in the brick wall at the far end and opened it. Another space, equal in size to the first.

'I reckon that the loft over the props room is through there.' He indicated an access hatch in the wall at the far end. 'The roof dips right down at that end of the building so it's probably just crawl space through there.'

He walked over to the hatch, bending down. 'I smell something.' He tugged at the hatch and it didn't budge.

'Want a hand?'

'That's okay. Hold the torch, will you?' Lucas squared up to the hatchway and pulled hard. When it gave he almost fell backwards, and the distinct smell of patchouli started to leak through the opening.

His mouth was obscured by the mask, but in the torchlight his eyes were smiling. 'We're getting warmer.'

He angled the beam of the torch through the hole. Beyond it, Thea could see the underside of the roof, sloping downwards. 'There's the extract vent.'

'Yeah, and it looks pretty filthy. See those slipped slates? I reckon that the air's being extracted from the building and then leaking back inside through that hole.'

'That's one half of the puzzle.' Thea bent down beside him, shining her torch beam over the rest of the space, and suddenly recoiled. 'Ugh!'

'What?' He steadied her, putting himself in between her and the access hatch.

'I think it's a rat's nest.' Thea shivered, looking around in case anything was headed towards her.

'All right.' He kicked the hatch closed, his hand finding hers. 'We're going back now.'

It was clear what Lucas had on his mind. Darkness and rats. He knew they reminded her of that police cell in Bangladesh.

'Don't you want to see?'

'I'll come back up later.' He was holding tightly onto her hand, pulling her back, away from the one thing that she knew he was desperate to see.

'Thinking of taking the credit all for yourself, are you?' There was no point in telling him not to come back—telling Lucas not to do anything was like a red rag to a bull. And he wasn't going into that crawl space on his own.

He turned slowly. In the silence she could hear a scrabbling sound coming from somewhere. 'You don't have to do this, Thea.'

She took a step towards him. Just having him close gave her courage. 'I do, actually.'

He nodded. 'Okay. Stay here, then.' He left her a few paces away from the hatch and bent to open it then crawled through. Thea shuddered, keeping her torch beam on the opening.

Something darted out of the hatchway, a small shadow running along the bottom of the wall and off into some dark corner. Thea heard herself whimper but she didn't run. She wasn't alone here.

She could see the torch beam inside the cramped space, and finally Lucas emerged, his face thankfully not bitten off by rats. 'We've done it, Thea.'

'Good. Come away from there now. Shut the hatch.'

For once he did as he was told. 'Rats gnaw everything. The sealed intake vent for the props room is through there, and it's got a hole as big as my fist in it.'

'Ugh. So we were breathing patchouli oil and rat droppings in there.'

'Yeah. And Derek was breathing airborne tuberculosis infection. Probably for hours every evening for a couple of weeks.'

Thea shivered. 'That's really gross.'

'Yeah, this place is going to be jumping tomorrow. Pest-control officers, ventilation engineers.' His eyes were shining and she couldn't help but smile. 'There's our answer, though.'

'You did it, Lucas.'

'No. We did it.'

Thea stayed close to him as they made their way back to the door at the head of the stairs, and as soon as she was back through it she heaved a sigh of relief. They shed their gloves and masks, found the caretaker, and told him he could lock up for the night.

'I suppose we'll be following through on any potential risks here and doing some more testing.'

'Yep. Although the testing will probably be at the London City Hospital. They serve this area.'

He had the boot of his car open, putting the gloves and torches back, and Thea was glad that he couldn't see the disappointment that must be written all over her face. There was no *we* about this really. Her job remained in one place, at the hospital. Lucas worked wherever he was needed. Just as surely as they'd been thrown together, they were being pulled back apart, like small boats bobbing on the waves.

'Have you eaten yet?'

'No. But I'm really tired and I've got some things to do tonight. If you could just drop me home?' Suddenly, this wasn't the happy ending she'd thought it would be. It was just another ending between her and Lucas, and she didn't want to drag it out over dinner.

'Yes, of course. Another night maybe?'

Thea gave the brightest smile she could muster. 'Yes. Maybe.'

CHAPTER FIFTEEN

THERE WAS STILL Mumbai. Thea wasn't sure about how she felt about it on any level, going with Lucas, delivering a paper that she was sure wasn't good enough, or stepping out of the warm safety of home and going back to Asia. All of it was too much to think about. But in amongst all of the dread she was excited as well.

She went up into the loft and took down the box of clothes she'd brought back from Bangladesh. Some of them were old and worn, but others delighted her unexpectedly. Loose, comfortable trousers and bright tops. Thea washed and ironed them carefully, and put them along with the clothes she'd bought for the trip.

Lucas was tanned and relaxed from his holiday in the South of France with Ava. They were travelling together, and from the moment he picked her up at her house to the moment that the porter opened the door of her hotel room, he never left her side. Not that he'd crowded her, but he was always there. And Lucas had always been good company and a great travelling companion.

At the evening reception he complimented her on her dress and somehow managed to keep a respectable distance at the same time as never quite being out of sight. It was odd. Not at all like Lucas to be half there, he never did anything by halves.

When she woke up alone in the large hotel bedroom,

which could have been practically anywhere in the world, she felt a strange sense of longing. She'd promised herself that nothing was going to happen with Lucas on this trip, and it appeared that it was going to be easier to keep that promise than she'd anticipated. It had been almost a shock when he'd bidden her goodnight and turned away without even a glance behind him.

At breakfast, she found out why. The chatter at the tables was about the conference, the people there and the medical issues that were to be discussed. And who had slept with whom last night.

'It's always the same.' Lucas grinned at her as they were finishing their coffee. 'Most people come to a conference to learn something and make contacts who'll help them in their work. But there's always the odd one or two who reckon that it's a good opportunity for some extra-curricular activities.'

And those were the one or two who were gossiped about relentlessly. 'But that's not you, is it?'

'Nope.'

'Or me.'

He leaned across the table towards her. 'Definitely not. The only opinion anyone's going to be voicing about you is how great your paper is.'

And that was the end of it. They fell into a warm companionship, working together, eating together and snatching as many moments as they could to leave the hotel and see a little of Mumbai. It didn't even seem to matter that it was driving her crazy, being so close to him and yet unable to touch him at night, because Thea could sense that it was driving him crazy, too.

Lucas's resolution not to be seen anywhere near Thea's room lasted for two full days. Then, at two in the morning, his phone woke him up.

'Ava?' He'd gone to bed last night thinking about Ava.

He knew that she was perfectly safe and happy with his parents, but Lucas felt slightly guilty that he wasn't there to make sure that she was safe and happy.

'No. It's Thea. Were you asleep?'

The strained tone of her voice removed any temptation to tell her that, of course, he'd been asleep. 'No, I was…' He couldn't think of anything he might be doing at two in the morning other than sleep.

'You were. I'm sorry…'

She was apologising again. Always a bad sign. 'You called me at two in the morning to ask if I was asleep?'

'No, I…' The sound of her weeping quietly came down the line, and Lucas regretted the frustration that had crept into his voice. Tucking his phone under his chin, he pulled on his clothes.

'Hey. None of that. Tell me what's up.'

She gave a short, self-deprecating laugh. 'I'm just being stupid, that's what. Go back to sleep.'

'Before I do, you'd better tell me what you're being stupid about.' Lucas noiselessly opened the door of his room, his footsteps in the corridor muffled by the thick carpets.

'Oh, you know. Stage fright.' She sighed. 'I think I took on a bit more than I can handle. I've been lying awake, trying to think of all the ways that I can get out of tomorrow. I'll be okay.'

No, she wouldn't. If Lucas knew Thea at all, he knew that she wouldn't have called in the first place if she'd thought she was going to be okay. And if she lay awake the whole night, not only would she be even more tired and distressed in the morning, she might just come up with a way to get out of presenting her paper.

'Want some company?'

'No, really—room service is bringing a cup of tea and I'll drink that and then go back to bed. Hold on a minute, I think that's them now. I just need to put some clothes on…'

Lucas closed his eyes, leaning his forehead against

the door. If he'd known she wasn't dressed, he could per-haps have dragged the conversation out a little longer and enjoyed the mental picture.

She opened the door, wearing a T-shirt and sweatpants, her phone slipping from where she'd tucked it under her chin and dropping to the floor when she saw him.

'Are you going to let me in, then?' She hesitated, and Lucas gave his most persuasive grin. 'Before anyone sees me?'

She wiped her tear-stained cheek with her hand. 'You didn't need to...' As soon as he closed the door behind him she gave up the seemingly gargantuan effort of pretence that she'd been making. 'Thanks, Lucas.'

'No trouble. I was awake anyway, my phone rang. Per-haps they'll bring enough tea for two.'

'I ordered a pot. Just one cup, though.'

'I'm sure we'll manage.' Her room revealed her state of mind, even if her words didn't. Papers spread out on the red and gold cover of the large bed. Three different outfits, the hangers hooked over the top of the open door of the wardrobe. There was no furrow in the carpet from where she'd paced up and down, between the window and the bed, but if Lucas knew her at all, that was exactly what she'd been doing.

'Wondering what to wear?' He decided to address her worries one at a time.

She nodded. 'Yeah, I was thinking this one...' She picked up the sleeve of a dark jacket, which went with a pair of sludge-coloured trousers.

'Boring. And you'll get really hot in that. What about this?' Lucas peered into the wardrobe, pulling out a pale, silky top. 'With this.' He caught sight of a flash of colour and extricated one of her seemingly endless selection of wide scarves.

'You think so?' She looked uncertainly at the two as he held them together. 'The colours do go.'

'Yeah, and if you wear it with dark trousers, you'll look great.'

She frowned at him. 'This is a professional conference. I don't want to look great.'

'You mean you don't want anyone to look at you. Sweetheart, they're going to be doing that anyway. You may as well look nice.'

She gave a shrug and began to search unenthusiastically through the contents of the wardrobe. It looked as if she'd over-packed for this trip, and brought enough clothes for a month. Lucas supposed that it gave her the option of picking out something to wear for the next day and then changing her mind at the last moment.

'This, you mean?' She'd put the top onto the hanger along with a pair of dark blue trousers, and twisted and knotted the scarf around the shoulders.

'Perfect.' Lucas grinned with approval. 'You'll look lovely.'

'I don't *want* to look lovely.'

'And very professional.'

His words seemed to mollify her a little. She put the sludge-coloured outfit back in the wardrobe, hooking the new outfit over the top of the door, and Lucas heaved a sigh of relief. 'I'll hang this there, and think about it.'

She jumped as a quiet knock sounded on the door. Lucas stepped back instinctively, out of sight of anyone standing in the corridor, while she accepted a tray and sent the waiter away.

'Plenty for two.' She set the tray down on a small table by the window, smiling nervously. Lucas waved her into a seat and poured her a cup and she took a sip, watching as he collected the papers up from the bed into one pile.

'How many times have you been through this?' He sat down opposite her.

'Too many. Each time I do it, it seems worse than the last.' She passed him the cup and he took a sip.

'Why don't you leave it for tonight? Get some sleep and we'll go through it together over breakfast when you're fresh.'

She agreed just that little bit too quickly. 'Yeah. You're right. Thanks, Lucas.'

That was his cue to leave. And as soon as he did, she'd probably get that horrible outfit back out of the wardrobe and start fretting over her papers again until dawn broke and she realised that only coffee and good luck was going to get her through the morning. Lucas wasn't going to let that happen.

'I'm going to practise one of my new techniques on you first, though.'

The idea of Lucas and a new technique did the impossible, cutting through the heavy mess of worry that was lying on her chest like a stone. 'What are you going to do?'

'Wait and see. I want you to lie down on the bed.' He indicated the spot where the pillows were piled up to form a backrest.

Lying on the bed for a new technique? And Lucas's gorgeous smile, the one that she'd never been able to resist. 'Can I take my tea with me?' How dangerous could it be if you could drink a cup of tea at the same time?

He gave a nod and she picked up her cup and saucer, holding it in front of her like a defensive weapon.

'You don't need to worry.' He chuckled.

'What makes you think I'm worried?' She tilted her chin at him defiantly, but the damage was already done. The dark glint in his eye, the sudden feeling that his bulk was looming over her set her cup wobbling slightly in the saucer, and Thea steadied it with her free hand.

He watched as she set her tea on the nightstand and slid onto the bed, folding her arms over her stomach. Then he sat down at her feet.

'Close your eyes.'

Protesting would only make her look as if she thought
something was about to happen. Thea squeezed her eyes
shut.

'And relax.'

'I'm relaxed.'

He didn't even bother to answer. Lucas's soft chuckle
told her that he knew full well that her whole body was as
tight as a bowstring. When she felt his fingers brush against
her bare toes, she started involuntarily.

He took hold of one foot, his touch light but purpose-
ful. It was nice enough, but it was her head that needed to
be worked on, not her feet.

'Do you have any rose oil?'

He knew she always travelled with at least one small
bottle of soothing oil, and rose oil had always been her favourite. Once upon a time, in a land far away, it had been
one of the sweet smells of their lovemaking.

Thea opened her eyes and sat up. 'No, I have lavender
oil. Will that do?'

'Perfect. Stay there.'

When he collected the oil from the dresser, he switched
a lamp on, turning out the main light. He threw open the
heavy curtains, letting the darkness in. Lucas wasn't afraid
of the dark the way that she was.

'Lucas?'

'Nothing's going to hurt you.' He lifted her feet to put
a towel under them and tipped a little of the oil into his
palm, rubbing his hands together to warm it. The smell of
lavender did little to calm her.

His hands again, rubbing gently. Missing nothing, the
sensitive skin in the arches of her feet, her ankles. Lucas
was concentrating on his task in silence. Gradually a feeling of well-being began to suffuse her whole body.

'That's it.' He leaned forward, picking up her hand, and
she realised that it had slid from her stomach to her side.

He massaged her palm, sending warm shivers all the way up her arm.

'Where did you learn this?' Even her voice seemed to have relaxed into a low whisper.

'I went to a class with my dad. When Mum was ill.'

'And it made her feel better?' Thea tried to call to mind the studies she'd read about massage and illness, and decided that she could do that some other time. The warmth of his hands, the delicious smell, the way he seemed to be touching her whole body was a powerful drug.

'Not the massage. He wasn't all that good at it. But she really appreciated him going; it was a bit of a departure for him. My father's always been a proponent of measurable cause and effect.'

'And you're not.' Lucas knew all about the magic of touch. The subtle rhythms of the human body that defied any attempt to categorise them.

'I'm a proponent of both. Science is important. What's going on in someone's head is important too. I thought we agreed on that.'

The world in which they had to talk about anything, to work out whether they agreed or disagreed, seemed a long way away. Here it was just his hands. Like sex, only... Only without the consequences. You didn't wake up the next morning hating yourself because someone had rubbed your feet the night before. You didn't have to worry about contraception or what the world thought. It was just feet.

'Roll over.'

She obeyed him without a murmur. When he raised one foot, his fingers sliding along her calf, all she could think was that this was lovely. A sigh escaped Thea's lips.

'Good?' If she'd been able to see his face, she would have seen the tenderness that his voice betrayed.

'Yeah. Nice.' If he'd rolled her over again, and stripped off her T-shirt and sweatpants, she would have done nothing to resist him. But she knew that he wouldn't. When she felt his fingers at the small of her back, she gave herself up to him as completely as if he'd been inside her, warmth spreading from the cluster of nerve endings and making the tips of her fingers tingle.

'You've got a knot, there.' His fingers concentrated on a spot in the middle of her back, pressing hard, and Thea felt her own momentary resistance before the muscles relaxed. His fingers pressed a little harder, and her gasp drew a grunt of approval from him. He explored the spot a little more and then moved on to the next vertebra.

Lucas knew how to arouse and he wasn't employing any of the tricks that would have made her cry out for him. He wanted something different from that and he'd got it. Her body felt as if it was floating, warm and weightless. Far too relaxed to want anything other than this moment.

She felt his lips brush her back, and then he pulled her T-shirt back down. The pressure of two fingers on her shoulder was more than enough, and her body obeyed him, rolling over.

'Don't get up yet. Just relax for a moment.' He slid the towel out from under her feet and covered her with the counterpane. The last thought that drifted through Thea's head was that she'd just stay here for a minute longer before she finished her tea.

She was asleep. Curled up on the bed, her breathing soft and regular. Lucas thought for a moment about undressing her and decided that the night was not so hot that it was a necessity. In any case, that was much too much to expect of himself. His body was already raging with an intense need and he couldn't stand much more of it.

Quietly he closed the curtains. The lamp glowed in the corner of the room, and he decided to leave it on in case she woke later on. Temptation roared through his veins and he reminded himself that if he lay down beside her tonight, there was always a chance that someone would see him leaving in the morning and they'd become the latest victims of the conference gossip machine. The thought propelled him towards the door. He opened it an inch, looking outside to make sure that no one was in the corridor, then walked quickly back to his own room.

Thea found Lucas on the covered veranda, drinking coffee and watching the rain. The breeze meant that the air was cool and fresh. A perfect morning.

'You slept well?' He grinned at her as she sat down in the other wicker chair at his table.

'Yes, thanks. I woke up this morning feeling calm and relaxed and reeking of lavender.'

He chuckled. 'The technique worked, then.'

'It certainly did. You'll have to teach me some time.'

He shot her a thoughtful look, as if last night was then and this morning was now. 'When we get home maybe. Would you like me to go through your talk with you?'

'Thanks, but no. I've been through it about a million times already. I'd rather just have a moment of calm before I have to enter the fray.'

He nodded approvingly. 'If you want, I can work the laptop to display the images. Let you concentrate on what you have to say.'

She wished he'd said that sooner. It would be great if she could just do the presentation and have someone else work the laptop, but he didn't know which image went with which part of the talk. 'It's too complicated.'

'I've got the script you sent me. I read through it on holiday. The prompts are all in there.' He grinned. 'I haven't been through it a million times, but I'm fairly au fait with it.'

Something in his look told her that he knew every word of her talk. While she'd been stressing over her presentation, he'd been quietly working through it, weaving a fine safety net under her that she'd not seen but was nonetheless there.

'Thanks. I'd really like that.' She leaned back in her chair and Lucas beckoned one of the waiters, who seemed to know either by instinct or long practice when to appear and when not to interrupt. Watching the rain softly plashing on the great leaves in the garden seemed as if it was all she needed to do right now.

CHAPTER SIXTEEN

THE MORNING'S SESSION was a comparison of how people all over the world were facing the challenges of TB. Delegates from the US and Europe spoke, and then it was Thea's turn. Walking to the podium with Lucas at her side somehow didn't seem so excruciating as she'd thought it might be.

He sat down quietly at the small side table reserved for data projection. She glanced at him and he smiled and nodded. *Go for it.*

She began to talk, dimly aware that images were flashing up on the screen behind her. When she turned to refer to a graph, showing the comparative numbers of incidents of TB in the UK over the last ten years, it was there already, completely on cue. Thea began to forget the sea of faces in front of her and concentrated on speaking to individuals, a woman in a green sari in the fourth row, a man who was sweltering in a suit, almost at the back.

Before she knew it, she was on the last page of her script. When she'd finished, and polite clapping turned to whole-hearted applause, she wanted to stay right where she was and talk some more. Maybe read the whole thing again, with a few variations.

Lucas was at her side. 'Leave them wanting more,' he whispered quietly in her ear, and escorted her off the stage. Perfectly mannered, as if she were the star of the show. Suddenly she felt as if she was.

'Enjoy it?' he murmured in her ear as they took their seats in the front row of the auditorium, ready for the next delegate.

Thea nodded, and he chuckled. She was aware that she was grinning stupidly, but couldn't stop.

The next few minutes wiped the smile off her face.

In the sparkling haze of achievement she hardly heard the announcement that the delegate from Bangladesh had been unable to come to the conference due to family commitments, and that a colleague had flown in to deliver his paper. When that colleague walked onto the stage, it felt as if her blood had suddenly frozen.

For a moment she was unable to move, caught immobile as her limbs turned to ice. Getting up from her seat felt as if she was shattering joints that had lost the ability to flex and move, but she had to go. Had to get away from there.

She felt Lucas's hand on her arm, pulling her back into her seat. 'What's...?' He followed the line of her terrified gaze to the small, dapper man who was standing at the podium. 'You know him?'

His head twisted around as Dr Nair was introduced to the audience. Having worked for twenty years as the director of a TB clinic near Dhaka, he was now the head of research at an institute in the city. Understanding flashed in Lucas's eyes.

'Stay, Thea. Please.' His hand slid down her arm, and his fingers found hers.

'I...I can't.'

'You can face him, Thea. He should be the one who can't face you.' Lucas was leaning in close, speaking straight into her ear so she could hear him over the applause.

Dr Nair obviously didn't think so. He must have seen the list of speakers and his gaze found her almost immediately, hardening into frank dislike.

'Don't do it.' Lucas's words penetrated her panic.

'Don't do what?' Fear made her snap at him.

'Whatever it is you're thinking of doing. Just don't.'

That ruled out a whole slew of things. Running away. Crying helplessly. Letting the darkness rule her. Lucas's hand closed around hers and she stayed put.

All the same, it felt as if everything was crumbling around her. The applause that the auditorium had given her. All the work she'd done in the last five years.

The lights went down and his grip tightened. Dr Nair began to speak, and Thea took a deep breath. She could do this.

In between the panic, the presentation was fascinating. It made sense of much that she had learned, working in Bangladesh, clarifying the issues and suggesting a way forward. Dr Nair walked to his seat amidst a clamour of applause, managing to shoot her another disapproving look on the way.

The open questions part of the session got under way and Thea shrank into her seat, hoping that none of the questions would be directed at her. The first was in response to Dr Nair's closing comments, asking about the role of foreign aid in his work.

That prompted a long spiel about working together for common aims, educating each other... Thea concentrated on continuing to breathe. At the very last, just when she thought that she was doing a pretty good job of it, Dr Nair smoothly slid the knife in.

'Dr Coleman spoke about working with diverse communities in an urban setting. I would be interested on what she has to say about foreign aid workers respecting local cultures.'

The microphone was being passed towards her, like a cup of poison, moving inexorably closer. She heard Lucas spit out a curse and he reached across her to take the microphone.

She gave him an imploring look, aware that whatever she said to him was likely to be broadcast across the auditorium, and Lucas gave that bright, melting smile that always accompanied his picking up a challenge.

'I'd also be interested in what Dr Nair has to say about the balance between respecting culture and respecting the law...'

Enough. Before she could stop herself, Thea was on her feet, taking the microphone from him. Lucas had succeeded in what he was trying to do, deflecting the interest of the audience away from her and back onto Dr Nair. Ayesha's voice was being lost. Her own voice was being lost.

'I think that Dr West and Dr Nair are both missing the point. Of course it's imperative for us to respect both culture and the law, but as doctors we have a responsibility to everyone who comes to us for help. We must never lose sight of that fact either.'

She could feel the warmth of Lucas's grin next to her. A murmur of agreement went around the audience and she saw the woman in the green sari nodding. She took a deep breath and sat down again.

The conversation darted from one delegate to another, from one point of concern to the next. And slowly the feeling crept up on Thea. She wasn't finished yet.

Lucas was planning on hurrying her away as soon as the session was finished, but it seemed that Thea had other ideas. Before he could stop her she was out of her seat, walking towards where Dr Nair was standing, and all he could do was follow as closely as he could. As Thea approached him, Dr Nair gave her an irritated look.

She ignored that and held out her hand, her fingers trembling. 'Dr Nair, I know that we disagree, and I respect your opinion. I would like to shake your hand.'

'I think not.' Dr Nair turned his back on her.

Lucas took her firmly by the arm to walk her away in as dignified a manner as possible. She jabbed him in the ribs with her elbow.

'What the papers said about me, Dr Nair, wasn't true. I only meant to help Ayesha.'

Dr Nair turned. 'I stand by what I said then, Dr Coleman. You deserved everything that you got.'

Thea paled suddenly, backing away from him, and Lucas silently cursed the man. 'Come away, Thea. Now.' He bent to whisper the words in her ear but he was too late. A woman in a green sari had been standing nearby, listening quietly.

'I will shake your hand.' She extended her hand to Thea. 'And that of Dr West.'

The woman seemed to know him. Lucas tried to recall whether they'd been introduced in the course of the last few days.

'I am Dr Patel. I have been looking forward to meeting you.'

Lucas had been looking forward to this moment for some time, but had never thought it would come quite so soon or in quite this way. 'Dr Patel? It's a pleasure to see you here. I didn't expect you to come all this way in person.'

'I visit Mumbai from time to time. I had a trip scheduled and when your solicitor told me that you would be here, I decided to deliver the letter myself, rather than send it by courier.'

'Lucas? What's going on?'

He grinned. 'Dr Patel's the director of one of the largest TB clinics in Bangladesh.'

'And it appears that I have been conspiring with Dr West behind your back.' Dr Patel held out an envelope to Thea. 'I have a letter for you, from someone I think you know. It is in Bangla, but I can translate it for you if you wish.'

'My Bangla's pretty rusty…' Thea opened the envelope and a photograph fell out. She bent to pick it up, staring at it in disbelief.

'You recognise her?' Dr Patel smiled.

Thea looked again at the picture. A mother with her

three-year-old child. The little girl had dark curls and a bright, cheeky smile.

'I don't...' Thea let out a little scream and almost dropped the photo. Lucas felt her sag against him and he supported her to an empty seat.

'It's Ayesha.' There were bright tears in Thea's eyes as she turned her face up to him. 'Please, tell me it's her.'

'It's her.'

'But... Dr Patel, thank you so much. But how?'

Dr Patel sat down next to her. 'Dr West has been making enquiries on your behalf. He engaged a solicitor in Bangladesh, who traced Ayesha to my clinic.'

'She's ill?'

'Ayesha is well. So is her child. She works at the clinic.'

Thea looked at the photograph again then held it to her heart, her hands clasped over it as if it was the most precious thing in the world. 'Thank you. Thank you so much.' Tears spilled from her eyes. 'Look, Lucas. Look at her little girl. She's so pretty.'

Lucas thought that he had already shared everything there was to share with Thea, but he couldn't have been more wrong. This moment was new, and more precious than diamonds.

Dr Patel was laughing as Thea turned to her, a barrage of questions on her lips. 'Yes, she is happy, and so is her child. She finished her schooling at the women's shelter and applied to work at my clinic. She tells me that her choice of career is in no small part inspired by the woman doctor who helped her escape her husband. She works as a ward auxiliary, but she studies also. Her dream is to become a qualified nurse.'

'Oh.' Thea's hand flew to her mouth. 'She did it. She told me that she wanted to be a nurse. Does she need anything? Does she need books, or help with tuition fees?' She broke off, her attention suddenly caught by something behind Lucas. When he turned to see what it was, he saw Dr Nair staring at them.

He must have heard. Thea straightened, meeting his gaze. There were no words, but it was Dr Nair who looked away first. Despite the group of people who had gathered to talk to him, he turned and hurried out of the auditorium.

'Who's right, Lucas? Dr Patel or Dr Nair?' Dr Patel had excused herself, to speak to one of the other delegates, but she had promised to join Thea and Lucas for tea later. Thea sat, unable to take her eyes off the photograph of Ayesha.

'I think Dr Patel's right. I think that we all have to preserve the good things about our own societies and change what's bad.' He shook his head. 'But it's what you think that matters. Was what you did wrong?'

It was the question she'd asked herself again and again, and had never been able to answer. Now she could. 'If I had it all to do again, I'd do it. Being locked up, being shouted at and vilified. It was all worth it just to be able to see this photograph. I know I did the right thing. Ayesha wouldn't have survived much longer if she'd stayed with her husband.'

'There's your answer.'

'I'm so happy, Lucas. I can never thank you enough for all you've done.'

He smiled. 'Why don't you read your letter?'

'Not here. Can we go somewhere quiet? I want to read it to you.'

People were still leaving the auditorium and Lucas guided Thea through the crush of people in the lobby and into the lift. Suddenly they were alone.

He reached for her, catching her hand in his and drawing it slowly to his lips. Maybe it was the movement of the lift that propelled her into his arms. Maybe it was just that the world was tilting and Lucas was the only constant thing she could find.

'Where are we going?'

'No idea. You were the one standing by the lift buttons.' He wrapped his arms comfortably around her waist.

Thea twisted to see the floor indicators. 'Penthouse lounge.'

'Good plan. You can read your letter to me over lunch.'

'Thank you, Lucas.'

He smiled. 'Thank *you*. I wouldn't have missed this morning for the world.'

'I really wish we could stay for another week.' The taxi that had brought them to the airport had disappeared and as they walked together into the cool of the building it finally struck Thea that they were going home.

'Which would you choose, though? More conference days or a holiday?'

Thea thought carefully. 'Two weeks, then. It'll have to be two. Another week at the conference and then a holiday.'

Lucas chuckled. 'Yeah. It's been inspiring, hasn't it?'

In so many ways. 'I want to come back. I want to see more of India than just a hotel room and a conference suite. And I want to take Dr Patel up on her offer. I'd love to visit her clinic and to see Ayesha again.'

'You will.' Lucas stopped suddenly, his gaze on the boards that listed flight departures. 'We're going to have to check in now. We're a bit late.'

They'd dawdled through breakfast and taken a last stroll through the hotel gardens. The hotel concierge had practically bundled them both into the taxi, clearly disapproving of their reluctance to leave. But now, in the anonymous crush of the airport, it felt as if they were already gone from India, and it was time now to hurry back to whatever England might bring.

Lucas strode towards the check-in desk, leaving Thea with the suitcases while he joined the queue. The process seemed a protracted one, and she smiled at a woman who had sat down next to her and was cradling a sleeping baby.

'You're going to London?' The woman was holding a pair of tickets, and Thea recognised the thick black code letters in the corner.

'I hope so.' The woman grimaced. 'Looks as if there's a problem. We can do without this.'

'What's happening?' When Thea glanced towards the check-in desk, the queue had disintegrated into a crowd.

'Overbooking, I think. My husband's trying to sort it out, we need to get on a flight today.'

'They must give you priority, surely. With the baby...'

The woman shrugged. 'I don't think that makes any difference. And Sara's not really the problem. We live in Mumbai so we can just go back home if we don't get a flight. My sister's getting married on Saturday, though. This'll be the first time my family have seen Sara.'

'Look, my friend's just on his way back. He might know something.'

As Lucas hurried towards them, a man standing behind the check-in desk started to make an announcement in Marathi, which was drowned out by groans of dismay from those who understood. As he repeated it in English, the queue started to break up.

'What's up?' Thea looked up at him.

'A couple of flights have been overbooked. Stay there, I'll be back...' Lucas was gone again, hurrying through the crowds, obviously sure of where he was going.

Another night in India. In an airport hotel, probably, but things could be worse. Thea turned to the woman next to her. 'Guess we'll just have to wait.'

It was half an hour before Lucas returned and by that time Thea was holding Sara, wishing she would wake up so that she could feel the tiny body move against her. 'What's happening?'

Lucas grinned. 'Hey, there, sweetie.' The greeting was for Sara. Despite having slept soundly through the noise and bustle of the airport, Sara seemed to decide that now was the time to open her eyes, and her hand reached for the thin cotton material of Thea's shirt, clutching it tightly.

Sara looked up at his smile and her eyes began to swim with tears. Thea rocked her gently, turning so the child could see her mother, feeling the sharp, instinctive tug as one small hand wandered towards her breast.

'What's...?' She swallowed hard. 'What's going on?'

'I've got vouchers for a different flight in an hour's time. We have to get to the flight desk to exchange them and then check in, so you need to give this little one back.'

He nodded towards Sara's mother, who was talking quietly into her phone. The woman started to shake her head slowly, tears forming in her eyes. 'No... No, it's okay. We'll get there, and if we don't... I don't know, but it'll be okay... Yeah, come back here.'

Thea looked up at Lucas. 'She's going to London, for her sister's wedding. She can't miss it.'

The woman had put her phone back into her bag and was wiping tears from her face, trying to smile. 'It's not the end of the world.' She reached for Sara. 'You have tickets, though? You'd better go.'

Thea shot an imploring look at Lucas and he reached inside his jacket. 'Here.' He put an envelope bearing the airline's logo into the woman's hand. 'Where's your husband?'

'He's coming back here.' The woman stared at the envelope as if it had suddenly floated down from heaven into her lap, then offered it back to Lucas. 'But I can't... You can't.'

Lucas shrugged. 'Yes, we can.'

The woman gave up on Lucas and tried Thea. 'Really, we'll be okay.'

'Take them, please. You can't miss your sister's wedding, and little Sara needs to see her grandparents. I want you to take them.'

The woman hesitated, and then clutched the envelope to her chest. 'Thank you. I don't know what to say.'

'Just call your husband, and tell him we'll meet him at the flight desk.' Thea stood up. 'Come on, Sara, you're going to London.'

They'd seen the couple through the departure gates and the woman had kissed Thea. She still didn't know her name, and the woman didn't know hers, but a hastily scribbled note gave the name of her husband's brother, who lived in Mumbai, and his phone number.

'I suppose we could call the number. We need to find a hotel if we're not going to get a flight today.'

'Could do.' Lucas looked up from his phone, which had been holding his attention on and off for the last ten minutes now. 'Or we could do this.'

He handed her his phone. On the small screen she saw a picture of a comfortable bedroom, tastefully decorated in the ornate style of India.

'That looks nice. Where...?' Thea swiped her finger across the screen for more details. 'This is in Delhi!'

'Yep. There are a couple of rooms available as late bookings, and flights go pretty much every half-hour from here. And it's only a couple of hours to—'

'The Taj Mahal.' Thea narrowed her eyes at Lucas and he grinned.

'Don't you want to see one of the seven wonders of the world?'

Of course she did. Going to a world-famous monument to love with Lucas, on the other hand, was something that needed careful and lengthy consideration. All of the risks. All of the temptations.

'Or we could find a hotel in Mumbai for tonight and go home tomorrow. That'll give you three whole days to get ready to go back to work on Monday.' Thea's heart sank at the thought. If Lucas was bluffing, he was making a great job of it.

'As against dropping out of circulation and visiting the Taj Mahal.' Risky and tempting was sounding more and more delicious by the moment.

'Yep. That's the choice.'

She grinned up at him. 'Let's do it.'

CHAPTER SEVENTEEN

THE HOTEL WAS thirty minutes' hectic taxi ride from the airport, and they arrived hot and wide-eyed. The monsoon had turned arid countryside into green hills, cloaked in mist at the tops, and the vivid colours of flowers and saris were everywhere.

In comparison the hotel was quiet and cool. They were welcomed with garlands of sweet-smelling flowers and led up the stairs and through a succession of arches and small lobbies, each of which served two or three rooms, finally stopping at an intricately carved door.

'Is this my room?' The porter had opened the door and was depositing Thea's luggage inside.

'Looks like it.' Lucas grinned, running his hand over the golden wood. 'Fabulous door. Is twenty minutes enough time to get settled?'

'Yes, I'll call you. I'd love to explore this place.' The hotel was a maze of walkways and balconies, not quite grand but quietly opulent.

'Me too. I'll see you later.' He waited outside as Thea accepted her key from the porter and walked through the beautiful door.

Thea took the garland of flowers from around her neck, hanging them across the ornate mirror of the dresser. Laying a long, wrap-around skirt that she'd bought in Mumbai onto the bed, along with a loose cotton top, she made for the shower. After ten minutes the warm water began to chill a little and she wrapped herself in a towel, rubbing at her wet hair.

The smells of India. They ranged from exhaust fumes, sweat and the sickly smell of decay to the scents of jasmine, frangipani and incense. Here it was the cool smell of leaves after the rain, which wafted into her room through the open windows, as muslin curtains blew in the breeze.

Lucas. Just the thought of him was intoxicating. Lost here, in this far corner of the world with him. Thea picked up her phone and dialled his number.

'Hey, there.' He sounded as relaxed as she felt. *'Are you ready?'*

She was ready. It had been a long journey, and it wasn't just miles they'd covered together. But she was finally at her destination and she knew what she wanted now. 'Where are you?'

'Take a look outside your window.'

She battled the billowing muslin curtains and walked through the glazed doors out onto a balcony. Not so much a balcony as an open corridor, which looked down on a small courtyard, planted with trees and flowers. Lucas was down there, dressed all in white.

'What are you doing down there?' Exploring, no doubt. Lucas could never resist that.

'Waiting for you to let down your golden hair.'

She could see his face, tipped up towards her, and she smiled down at him.

'Sorry, not long enough.' He was different. And so was she.

'Just as well there are stairs, then.' He disappeared for a moment and Thea leaned over the stone balustrade to see what he was doing. In the corner of the courtyard an open-sided stone staircase ran up the side of the building. When he got to the third floor he disappeared for a mo-

ment and then reappeared from an opening twenty yards
from where she was standing.

'That's very neat. Is this the only way you can get down
there?' Thea peered over the edge of the balcony.

'The restaurant on the ground floor leads onto the courtyard.'

'Architecture for lovers.' Thea could imagine a young
man slipping into the leafy courtyard at night and climbing the moonlit steps to his lover's balcony. The thought
made her smile.

His gaze was on her face. They both knew what was
about to happen. They'd known all along but they'd come
here anyway. Thea backed into her room and he followed,
closing the balcony doors behind them and snapping the
locks tight.

'Come here.'

There was no hesitation, no questioning when he took
her into his arms and kissed her. It felt so natural, as if this
was where she was supposed to be, and everything else
was just artifice. His body was hard, unyielding and she
wanted him now. Right now.

She reached down and her trembling fingers felt in his
trouser pocket. Nothing.

'Other one.' He bent to kiss her neck, while she slid her
hand into the other pocket and found what she was looking for.

'Just one?'

'I've got some more in my room. I didn't want to appear over-confident.'

'Okay. Just under-provisioned.' One condom wasn't
going to get them very far.

'It's enough.' He pulled her against him hard and she
gasped. Kissed her hard, letting her feel his passion. Letting her know what was coming.

'Now, Lucas.' Before anything stopped them. There was
time for long and slow later. There was time for everything

else later, but they had to break the long years of being alone, which stood between them.

'Not yet.' His lips curved into a delicious smile, 'Soon, though.'

His fingertips trailed around her waist and then he slipped his hand between the folds of fabric of her skirt. He tugged hard at the fabric of her knickers and she heard them rip. 'You ready for me?'

His hand slid along the inside of her leg, and his fingers found the answer to his question. She was more ready for him than she could stand right now.

'Lucas.' He knew every part of her, every last tremor and every quickening. And he could use them all. She curled her fingers around the condom she'd taken out of his pocket and tugged at his belt with the other hand.

He chuckled, bending to kiss her forehead. 'Wait, my love. Wait.' His hand brushed against her breast and she cried out in frustration. 'First things first.'

He pulled back for a moment, undoing a couple of the buttons on his shirt and then losing patience and pulling it over his head. One hand reached for the ice bucket on the sideboard. Cold on her lips, followed by the heat of a kiss. Her body started to shake and he wound one arm around her waist, supporting her weight against him, trailed the ice cube along the line of her jaw and down her throat.

A soft melody of heat and cold played on her skin. Slowly he unbuttoned her shirt, unhooked her bra. The warmth of his mouth on hers, and icy shivers running down her spine.

'Thea.' He choked out her name, and this time he didn't resist when she undid his belt and zipper. Her skirt joined the growing pile of discarded clothes at their feet and then she was in his arms and he was carrying her to the bed.

She held him tight, feeling the delicious press of his body on hers. 'I've never forgotten how it feels to have you inside me, Lucas.'

He caught his breath and she felt his body harden. He was stronger, broader than he had been. Somehow more tender. 'I've never forgotten either. But I want you to let that go now. Feel it again for the first time.'

The one last trace of doubt fell away. It didn't matter if they couldn't re-create old memories. They were making new ones. 'Yes.'

She rolled the condom down over him, and he gasped at her touch. Then his weight was on her, pinning her down. He slid inside her, just an inch, and she groaned, feeling her whole body begin to quiver. Leaning on his elbows, he grasped her hands and she hung onto him tightly. He kissed her, sliding inside her as he did so, and she wrapped her legs around his waist, so she could move against him.

'I'm…' She couldn't stop it now.

'I know.' The way his body was trembling with every strong thrust told her that Lucas wouldn't be too far behind her. His fingers curled tightly around hers and he kissed her again.

When she came Thea thought for a moment she was going to black out. But she could feel him with her, his body tightening, convulsing along with hers. She looked up into his eyes and knew that she was finally home.

He woke with her in his arms in the early hours of the morning. It felt so good to know, once more, that everything was right with the world and that he was where he was supposed to be, with Thea curled up against his chest, fast asleep.

When he felt her stir, he found her hand and her fingers twined with his. He let her wake up and then dropped a kiss on her neck. 'You okay, honey?'

She laughed, and pulled his hand up to her lips to kiss his fingers. 'Why wouldn't I be?'

Good question. Last night they'd taken everything to the limit. Extreme passion, and extreme tenderness. There had been moments when Lucas had thought his body would break and his heart would burst, but somehow he was in one piece this morning. And still wanting her.

She moved lazily against him. 'What's the time?'

'Four o'clock. We don't have to get up for another hour or so.'

'And you're going to sneak back to your room again? It's not strictly necessary, you know. Tourist hotels usually turn a blind eye to unmarried couples sharing a room.'

'I know. I quite like the element of subterfuge, though.'

The previous evening, when hunger for each other had temporarily given way to the need to eat, Lucas had got dressed and slipped back to his own room via the balcony, showering quickly and emerging from the other door leading to the hotel corridor. Thea had emerged from her own room at almost the same moment, for all the world as if they'd been alone in their rooms, reading quietly or unpacking for the last couple of hours. Not touching her for the duration of a long, lazy meal turned the first brush of his fingers on her cheek, when they were alone again, into a confection of pleasure.

She chuckled. 'We wouldn't have lasted in Bangladesh. No fancy hotels to run away to.'

'No. But the two of us in Bangladesh… It was never going to happen, I didn't give it a chance.' The tattoo on his arm reminded him of that. Was reminding him now that Thea was too precious to be hurt again and that he had to go carefully. The idea of a forgiven past had overwhelmed those fears last night, but they were always waiting to return.

'I know. It doesn't matter now.' The friction of her body against his as she moved to kiss him brought his senses alive again.

'You're not even slightly angry with me?' He raised an eyebrow and she laughed.

'What? Angry sex? Remember that time when I was so furious with you that I made you sleep on the sofa?'

'I do.' His body was hardening just at the thought. 'And then you crept in while I was asleep and tied me up. It was terrible.'

'Not what you said at the time.'

Lucas chuckled, kissing her brow. 'What was that all about?' He could remember nothing about the argument and everything about the way she'd caressed his body, teasing him until he'd begged her to finish it, vowing that he'd never cross her again.

'No idea. Probably something that didn't matter.'

'It all matters, Thea. You keep me honest. Don't ever stop nudging me back into shape when I need it.'

'Nudging?'

'Wrenching. Twisting.'

'Kissing?' She brushed her lips against his.

'That I particularly like. You bring me joy, Thea. You always have.' He whispered the words into her ear and felt her snuggle against him.

'Lucas.' She murmured his name, and it was all he wanted to hear. That, and the little sound she made just before she came.

He reached across her for the little bottle of lavender oil on the nightstand, putting it in her hand. She took off the top, carefully dropping some into his palm. It was time to take things slowly.

Just before the dawn, as she broke in his arms, she said it. The words he felt in his heart but that he still felt he had no right to hear.

'I love you.'

They walked together silently along the wide pathway that led to the Taj Mahal. Not so much as the brush of a finger's touch. Thea wore a long skirt and a scarf slung around her shoulders in a gesture of respect for the place. She seemed

serene, almost ethereally lovely, and Lucas was proud to
be the one walking by her side towards the marble dome,
pale in the morning sunlight.

'It's beautiful.' Lucas knew she had a camera in her bag
but, unlike most of the tourists around them, her first instinct wasn't to take it out. Thea seemed to be content with
drinking in a moment that couldn't be captured digitally.

'Yes.' He slowed his pace and she fell into step beside
him. As she moved, the almost imperceptible scent of lavender floated towards him on the breeze.

They'd explored everything. Stopped to look at the detail
of the magnificent carvings and inlay work, marvelled at
the curve of the red and gold ceiling. The dome had turned
from pink against a clear morning sky to pure white as the
clouds had gathered and the last of the monsoon rains had
freshened the air and made the marble terraces sparkle. Finally shades of amber and red as the sun had begun to set,
reflections shimmering in the water of the reflecting pool.

'We missed the market.' Lucas was looking out of the
window of the minibus as they sped along the highway
back to the hotel.

'I'd rather have done what we did. You can't rush a place
like that.' Next time, maybe they'd see the market. Thea
dared to wonder if maybe she would see the Taj Mahal
again with Lucas, and resolved that if that wasn't to be,
she'd never come back here again.

'Yeah.' He stretched in his seat, stifling a yawn. 'You're
right. We'll have to come back to see the rest.'

She dozed for most of the two-hour journey back to the
hotel, and they ate a late supper together in the quiet dining room. Then up to her room to throw off her clothes,
shower and fall into bed.

The click of the latch on the balcony doors, and she
smiled.

'Okay, honey?' Lucas's body, curling around hers, warm and comfortable.

'Yeah. Sleepy.'

'I know. It's been a good day, hasn't it?' His fingers brushed her cheek, and he leaned over to kiss her forehead.

'A wonderful day.'

'Sleep now.' He twined his fingers around hers and Thea fell asleep, holding his hand to her heart.

CHAPTER EIGHTEEN

HE WAS SPRAWLED on the bed in the morning light, tangled in a sheet and sleeping soundly. The kind of image that you wanted to keep for ever, locked away in your heart in case the sunshine made it fade. Thea ran her finger lightly along his arm, careful not to wake him. The contour of his shoulder. The valleys and ridges of his biceps and triceps. Perfect. He was undeniably perfect.

The only mark on his body was the tattoo, and that was something he'd done out of love, to reassure a grieving child. When he was old, maybe the ink would have spread and it would blur a little, but it would still be a reminder that Lucas's heart was the truest she'd ever known. If only she could help him believe that. If only she could persuade him that all the good things in life were his to take, if he'd just reach out.

Today, though, he seemed determined to take them. A late breakfast and a lazy morning sitting in wicker chairs, watching the last of the monsoon rains.

After lunch, Lucas disappeared to find the hotel concierge and returned with a borrowed chess set, the pieces intricately carved from ebony and sandalwood, a Maharaja and Maharani presiding over warriors mounted on elephants and horses. They played once with Western rules and then a second time with Indian rules, gleaned from a book that the concierge had produced.

It had seemed a perfect day, but when she lay in her bed that night, waiting to see his shadow outside on the balcony, he didn't come. Maybe he was calling Ava. He'd said that he would after they ate. Thea drifted off to sleep, in the fond belief that he'd wake her when he slipped into bed beside her.

At breakfast, he looked tired. The one question that she wanted to ask had to wait until they were alone together, sitting on the balcony outside her room.

'You didn't come.' Maybe he'd fallen asleep.

'No, I...' He looked at her thoughtfully. Suddenly it seemed as if he was a million miles away. 'There's no easy way to say this, Thea.'

No. Not after just two nights.

'Just say whatever's on your mind.' Don't say it. Please, don't say it.

'I think we should...' He shook his head. 'I'm not going to make the same mistakes I made last time.'

She managed to breathe again. He hadn't said it. Not making mistakes was a good thing, wasn't it?

'We have to end it now, Thea. We can't continue together.'

For a moment she wondered what he was talking about. He sounded so cold, as if he was cancelling an ill-conceived business deal. 'But... What do you mean, Lucas? What's happened? Did you speak to Ava last night? Is she all right?'

'Ava's fine. I'm talking about you and me. These few days have been...'

'Don't say it, Lucas. Don't you dare say that these two days have been wonderful and then leave me. Don't.'

'Think about it, Thea. You want to travel some more, you've said it yourself. I can't do that, I have to be there for Ava. I'm not in a position to share my life with anyone, not right now.'

'Don't you mean that you're just too afraid? In case

something goes wrong?' Thea could have bitten off her own tongue. Why did she have to say that?

For a moment she thought he was wavering. For one sweet minute she thought she saw the warmth in his eyes that preceded a kiss.

'No, Thea.' He almost choked out the words. 'I won't do this again. I won't string you along, pretend to you that it's all going to work out and then pull the carpet out from under you. I did it once, and I won't do it again.'

'Lucas! That doesn't make any sense at all.' He was going to leave her, just in case he broke her heart. Didn't he know that she'd rather take her chances?

'It makes sense, Thea. There's a whole world out there. You need to spread your wings, find your place in life again. Maybe I do too.'

She was tempted to tell him that they were her wings and she'd do whatever she pleased with them. But nothing she said was going to change his mind. She'd seen that look before, and Lucas was deadly serious about this.

'You really mean it, don't you?'

'Yes, I do.'

Suddenly it hit her. History was repeating itself. They'd taken the risk, pushed their relationship to the limit, and Lucas was no more able to commit to her now than he'd been seven years ago.

She stood up, her legs shaking. 'I won't come after you, Lucas. Not this time.'

'I don't want you to.' He couldn't even look at her.

Thea turned and walked away from him, closing the balcony door behind her and locking it tight.

When Thea hadn't appeared for lunch, Lucas had sent one of the hotel's housekeepers up to see whether she was all right. He was told that she'd checked out three hours ago. Mad with worry at the thought of her travelling alone, he summoned the concierge, who gave him the number of

the flight he'd booked for her, and Lucas called a taxi and
went to the airport.

Her flight had already taken off. She'd done what he'd
told her to do, and now that she was gone she wouldn't be
back. All he could do was wait, and check that her flight
had landed on time in Mumbai, and that she had boarded
the flight to London.

The airport was a vast and lonely place. A sea of bobbing heads, and none of them was Thea's. But she was on
her way home. She'd be all right. He knew that he had done
the right thing.

CHAPTER NINETEEN

MONDAY MORNING. AND, of course, it was raining. India seemed a very long way away. Thea picked up her bag, let herself out of the house, and walked to the Underground. She'd spoken at a conference, confronted her fears, and with Lucas's help she'd won. She'd made love and then she'd cried. Now it was time to go back to work.

Day One: Lucas's writing on a patient's case notes.
Day Three: Do the patients *have* to keep asking where that nice Dr West is?
Day Five: Note for the weekend: write up conference notes for Michael.
One week: Surely the first week has to be the worst?
Two weeks: Still trying to stop thinking about Lucas. No success.
Three weeks:

The calendar on the kitchen wall showed a blank for the third week. That was just how Thea felt. Blank.

This weekend she'd do something. Maybe ring around to see if anyone wanted to go with her to the cinema on Saturday evening or drive up to see her parents on Sunday. Or both. As she didn't have much enthusiasm for either, perhaps that was pushing things a bit. On the other hand, she really did have to stop thinking about Lucas.

She left her umbrella in the porch, kicking off her shoes in the hallway and throwing her raincoat across the banisters. She padded into the kitchen, wondering whether she had any soup in the cupboard. She was exhausted from sleepless nights, and the summer was over now.

Glancing out of the window, she noted that the rain had stopped. And that there was a tent in the back garden.

'Lucas!' Her door keys slipped through her fingers and jangled onto the floor. What the hell did he think he was doing?

Light was glimmering from inside the tent. It actually looked rather inviting. Thea bit back the thought and marched back into the hall. High heels probably weren't the best choice of footwear for wet grass in the dark, but if she was going to be assertive—and she was—they'd give her a couple of extra inches to be assertive with.

When she got out of the back door she found a gangway, laid from the edge of the grass to the opening of the tent. First problem solved. She approached the tent, drawing herself up to her full height.

'Lucas!'

The tent flap opened and a blast of warm air from a portable heater hit her full in the face. He was wearing a dinner suit, which only made him look even more handsome than usual, and when he beckoned her inside she followed him, almost despite herself. 'How did you know it was me?'

'Who else is going to erect a tent in my back garden? With drapes and a chandelier and...' This really was too much. 'A chaise longue.'

He dipped his head in acknowledgement, as if she'd just paid him a compliment. 'Well, I'd rather you'd happened on the tent after a ride on a camel across the desert. But you weren't going to come to the desert with me, were you?'

'Damn right, Lucas.' She could feel tears in her eyes. Why did he have to make this so hard? 'And this is *my* garden. You're not to go putting up tents in it without my express permission. Which you don't have.'

In a minute the anger that had got her this far was going to give way to tears. She wanted him gone before that happened. Thea made a wild gesture in the direction of the back gate. 'You have to go. And you have to take all of this with you, even if it takes you all night.'

'Wait, Thea. There's something I want to show you.'

'No, I'm not going to wait. There's nothing I want to see. You made it perfectly plain to me where we stood in India. You said we had our lives to live, and that we should both spread our wings.'

'I am spreading my wings. I love you, Thea.'

She waited. 'And there's a *but* coming...'

'No. I love you. I'd camp in your back garden for the rest of my life if that's what it took.'

'Don't be ridiculous. What about Ava?'

'I might have to get a bigger tent. She's got a lot of stuff.'

'Lucas! Wake up. Smell the coffee or the flowers or whatever else is going to bring you to your senses.' This wasn't going the way that Thea had expected. She'd thought he'd hurt her so badly that she would never want to speak to him again. Until she saw him, the theory had worked perfectly, but now she wasn't only speaking to him, she was allowing herself to hope.

'I love you, Thea.'

Damn. He'd said it again. This time she couldn't stop the tears. And when Lucas stepped forward he was the only thing she had to hang onto. She let him steady her for a moment and then took a step back.

'What do I have to do to make you go away?'

'Listen to me now. I know this is my fault and that I've no right to ask anything of you, but I'm going to do it anyway.' There was one candle on the table beside the chaise longue that wasn't lit. He struck a match, holding it to the wick. 'Just for the time it takes for this candle to burn down to here.' He held his finger to a band that circled the candle, about a third of the way down.

'You can't just say ten minutes, can you? It has to be until a candle burns down, or sand runs out of a glass.' Thea couldn't help a wry smile.

He shrugged, shaking his head. 'No. Suppose I can't.'

There was something about his eyes. Imploring and yet determined. They both knew she couldn't hold out against that. 'Okay, then. Just until the candle burns down. And then you promise you'll go.'

'Promise. Sit down, won't you?'

The only place to sit was the chaise longue. Thea perched on the edge of it. She'd promised to listen, not recline.

'You have ten minutes, Lucas.'

Ten minutes. When he'd planned all this it had seemed more than enough to do what he had to do but now it seemed like nothing. He had to be quick. Lucas stripped off his jacket and tie and unbuttoned his shirt.

'What *are* you doing?' There was an expression of shock on Thea's face.

'I want to show you...' He pulled his shirt over one shoulder, and knelt down in front of her. When she touched his arm he winced in pain.

'You're having it lasered.'

'Just the birds. Ava's birthday stays.' The swifts at the top of the tattoo had almost disappeared now.

'It must hurt.'

He shrugged his shirt back over his shoulder, and put his jacket on. 'Yeah. Blue ink's not so bad as black but, yeah...it hurts.'

'Why?'

'Because when I got the tattoo I told myself that it was to remind me of you. But it was all a sham, a pretence that I still had some part of you. I don't want to pretend any more. I want you, Thea. I want to be with you and all the tattoo reminds me of is that we've spent too long apart. I can't even bear to look at it.'

She stared at him, hands clasped tightly in her lap.

'I do love you, Thea. I know I'm going to have to prove it to you, and I'm going to have to become the man I want to be. The one who won't hurt you, who'll take care of you.'

'You are that man.' She almost whispered the words.

'I look at you and I feel that I am.'

She was going to wake up in a moment. Find herself alone in her bed, and look out of the window to see only grass and a few shrubs in the back garden.

'Would you mind sitting down, please?' She patted the space next to her on the chaise longue.

The stress lines on his forehead began to melt and he sat down next to her.

'Thea, I know you're finding it hard to trust me right now, let alone love me.'

'I do love you, Lucas. I can't help it.'

'Isn't that a start? I wouldn't have done this unless I was sure, Thea. For a long time I used my responsibilities towards Ava as an excuse for not living my life. But when I saw you again...you helped me find my passion again. And then you helped me find the courage to change, to believe that I could love you and never let you down.'

The candle next to her guttered and flamed. Something clattered onto the table. It didn't matter. She'd given him ten minutes and he'd used it well. She would hear him out now.

'Time's up.' He seemed to be very interested in the candle.

'That doesn't matter now, Lucas. Forget it, I'm not going anywhere until we've sorted this out.' It might take all night. But she'd spent nights with Lucas in stranger places than a tent.

'It matters because...' He picked something up from the table, suddenly realising it was hot and bouncing it from one hand to the other. It sparkled in the candlelight. 'I didn't reckon on this getting caught in the flame. Obviously not my best moment when it comes to forward planning.'

'What *is* that?' He blew on the object in his palm and she saw. Lucas grinned, and slipped from his seat onto one knee in front of her.

'I've said what I want to say. And I want to offer this to you now. Not in the hope that you'll take it but to show you that I'm serious about this.'

'I...' She almost reached for the ring, but contented herself with just staring at it for a moment.

'I know. You have to think about it. I'll wait.'

She raised her eyebrows. 'What, you're not going to think about it with me?' This time she did reach out, tracing her fingers down the side of his cheek.

Slowly he leant forward. Brushed his lips against hers in an almost-kiss.

'Is that the best you can do?' Thea took his hand.

'I can do better.' This time he kissed her properly. All she wanted. All she needed. Right there.

'Are you expected home tonight?'

She'd thought his kiss was everything, but his smile was more. 'I was really hoping you'd ask that.'

CHAPTER TWENTY

FOR THE NEXT two weeks the ring was a constant part of Thea's life, turning up everywhere and anywhere. It sat on the mantelpiece at Lucas's house for a couple of days. It appeared in a glass of champagne when they celebrated the good news of Ava's Mantoux test results. She found it under her pillow when she woke in the morning and in her napkin when they went out to dinner together.

'You're going to lose this.' She held it up in the light of the chandelier, which had now been restored to its rightful place in the oak tree. It was beautiful. A single diamond, flashing with blue light, on a plain band.

'I keep my eye on it, wherever it is.' He turned his attention back to the map that was spread out between them. The canopy of the tree still sheltered them, even though the leaves were turning to gold and they had to wrap up warmly to enjoy the tree house now.

'So we go to Bangladesh first. To see Dr Patel and Ayesha.'

'Yes.' Thea hugged herself with excitement. 'And I'd like to spend some time at the hospital too. How do you feel about taking Ava with us?'

'She's asked me already about going. I said we'd wait and see but I don't see why she shouldn't come along. What do you think?'

'I think, if she wants to go, we should take her. We'll

both be there to keep an eye on her and make sure she's not confronted with anything too distressing.' One of the unexpected gifts that both Lucas and Ava had given her was to take it for granted that she should be a parent to Ava.

He nodded. 'Makes sense to me.' He dropped the pencil onto the map and it rolled towards the centre fold, where Thea's ring sat. 'There's something I want to ask you.'

'Fire away.'

'I was thinking…children.'

Thea had been thinking about that too. She wanted to have children, and Lucas's children would undoubtedly be a handful but they'd make her life complete. But if he didn't want that…

'What do you want?' She decided to play things cool.

'What do you want?' Apparently he'd made the same decision. Thea burst out laughing and he chuckled along with her.

'I just thought that…maybe Ava is enough for you.'

He shrugged. 'I guess after you've done it once you get into the swing of it. How many?'

'Four?'

'Four? I was thinking three…' He scratched his head. 'But four's a good number. I could work with that.'

'I was including Ava in my four.' She looked at him hesitantly.

'I love it that you did, sweetheart. So four, including Ava?' He picked up the pencil and added another cross to the map. 'I think we're definitely going to have to go back to the Taj Mahal. Maybe start work on number two of our four.'

'We'll go to the Taj Mahal. But we can wait for the children. It's a big thing for Ava to take on already, us getting married. If she sees me having a child straight away…' Thea wanted Ava to see her as an addition to her family, not someone who was taking Lucas away from her.

'I wouldn't worry. I found my mother teaching her to

knit the other day. They were like a pair of old ladies, both giving each other knowing looks.'

'What did you do?' Thea laughed.

'I told them that if and when we decide on anything we'll let them know. Preferably when junior's about six years old, so they don't have the opportunity to go out together and buy cute outfits.'

'I don't know. I quite like cute outfits.'

'So do I. That's why you and I are buying them.'

'There's always room for one more.' She leaned forward to kiss him. 'Always room for another one of those too.'

Suddenly his eyes were solemn. 'Okay, so you've admitted that we're going to get married. We're planning a baby and a holiday. There's something I need to do first.' He caught up her hand, watching her face intently.

'Do it. Do it now, Lucas.'

He slipped the ring onto her finger. 'No more dreams, sweetheart. Just realities.'

Reality was more than good enough. She leaned forwards and he kissed her. 'No more dreams.'

* * * * *

15_ST_10